THE
Bad Man

**Center Point
Large Print**

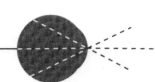

This Large Print Book carries the
Seal of Approval of N.A.V.H.

WAYNE D. OVERHOLSER

THE
Bad Man

CENTER POINT PUBLISHING
THORNDIKE, MAINE • USA

BOLINDA PUBLISHING
MELBOURNE • AUSTRALIA

This Center Point Large Print edition
is published in the year 2003 by arrangement with
Golden West Literary Agency.

This Bolinda Large Print edition
is published in the year 2003 by arrangement with
Center Point Publishing.

The text of this Large Print edition is unabridged. In other aspects, this book
may vary from the original edition. Printed in Thailand. Set in 16-point
Times New Roman type by Bill Coskrey and Gary Socquet.

US ISBN 1-58547-295-6
BC ISBN 1-74030-943-X

U.S. Library of Congress Cataloging-in-Publication Data.

Overholser, Wayne D., 1906-
   The bad man / Wayne D. Overholser.--Center Point large print ed.
     p. cm.
   Originally published in England under the name: Russ Thompson.
   ISBN 1-58547-295-6 (lib. bdg. : alk. paper)
     1. Large type books. I. Title.

PS3529.V33 B3 2003
813'.54--dc21

                                                        2002035122

                  Australian Cataloguing-in-Publication.
Overholser, Wayne D., 1906-
The bad man / Wayne D. Overholser.
ISBN 174030943X
1. Large print books.
2. Western stories.
I. Title.
813.6
         British Cataloguing-in-Publication is available from the British Library.

CHAPTER I

A L COBB was a bad man; he didn't pretend to be anything else. He laughed when he thought about it. Most people claimed to be good, and they'd be insulted if you called them bad. They went to church because they were good, and they read the Bible because they were good, and they forgot all about the Bible saying that no one was good but God.

Take the judge who had presided over his trial: Judge Jacob P. Charnley with his Prince Albert coat, and white goatee, and the great mane of hair that swept straight back from his forehead; Judge Charnley who was pledged by a solemn oath to give every man who came into his court an impartial trial and see that justice was done.

"I sentence you to hang by the neck until dead at high noon on August the first for the murder of Deputy Sheriff Lee Fawcett," Judge Charnley had said. "May God have mercy on your soul." Then he'd leaned forward and said in a voice so low that no one but Cobb had heard, "And by God, I never said those words with greater pleasure than I did just now. Lee Fawcett was my friend."

Then there was the Honorable Alexander H. Whipple, representative from Dead Horse County to the lower house of the legislature, and editor and publisher of the Dead Horse *Weekly Bugle*. Whipple was a little man with the overgrown ego of many little men. He dressed fastidiously, he wore a luxuriant growth of mutton chop whiskers, and he constantly chewed on a dead cigar which left a brown stain on both ends of his mouth.

Whipple had sat in the front row in the courtroom during the trial. After it was over and the sentence pronounced, Whipple had proceeded to his print shop and burst forth into a song of prose. Sheriff Fred Bentley had been all too glad to bring the first copy of the *Bugle* to Cobb that he could get his hands on.

"Read about yourself, Killer," Bentley said, grinning as he shoved the newspaper through the bars. "You made the headlines."

Cobb glanced at the newspaper and saw that he had indeed made the headlines: JUSTICE METED OUT, and below it the second line in slightly smaller letters, DEPUTY'S KILLER TO HANG. Cobb got up from his bunk and took the paper from the smirking law man and returned to his bunk. Ignoring Bentley, he read the long column.

"In all the annals of the West there has never been a more notorious bad man than Al Cobb: horse thief, stage robber, cattle rustler, bank robber, and murderer. On the lesser side, and perhaps not punishable by law, is the well-known fact that Cobb was a hired killer for certain interests who refused to settle their disputes by due process of law through the courts. No one besides God and Cobb know how many men fell before his smoking gun, but like the proverbial pitcher that went to the well too often, Cobb killed one man too many, our own beloved Deputy Sheriff Lee Fawcett. For this craven killing Cobb will hang at high noon on August 1."

There was more, much more, a little of it true, much of

it garbled, and most of it lies. But it made fine reading for the good people of Dead Horse County. They had lined the streets every morning, noon and evening when Cobb was moved from the jail, a small, brick building behind the courthouse, to the courtroom, or from the courtroom to the jail. And they had filled every seat in the courtroom and stood against the wall and lingered outside in the hall hoping to get a seat if one became vacant.

And then there was Ronald M. Purvis. Good old Ronnie Purvis. Whipple had interviewed him and Ronnie had given him a statement, brief but pointed. Ronnie said, "I grew up with Al Cobb in a small town in Nebraska. He was bad even as a boy. Everyone who knew him said he would come to no good end and would die at the end of a rope. That's exactly what he will do here in Dead Horse, Wyoming."

Cobb had laughed when he'd read it in the *Bugle*. He laughed now as he thought about it. That statement was so like Ronnie Purvis. But it was wrong. Not everyone who knew him said he would come to no good end and would die at the end of a rope. Not Janice Hart. Not Janice at all, although if it hadn't been for Janice, he wouldn't be where he was right now.

He stared upward at the long finger of light that fell across the cell from the little window near the ceiling, tiny specks of dust moving through it like live things. If he stood on the bunk and looked through that window, he could see the scaffold. Not that he wanted to see it. He'd be seeing it soon enough, but he knew it was there. It was finished. The trap had been tested. Everything would go like clockwork. Sheriff Fred Bentley had assured him of that. At least he didn't have to listen to the hammering, as he had when the scaffold was being built.

He looked at his watch: Ten o'clock. This was July 31. Twenty-six hours! It would be a Roman holiday at high noon tomorrow, with more than a circus and bread to offer the hungry public. Everyone in Dead Horse except maybe Ronnie Purvis would be on hand to watch the show. And Janice. No, Janice wouldn't be there, either. He smiled as he thought about her, and how it had started in the little Nebraska town of Royal.

CHAPTER II

AT sixteen Al Cobb was a junior in high school, one of the biggest and strongest boys in school, and certainly the boy with the worst reputation. He knew he had the reputation, although he wasn't sure how or why he had earned it. Maybe it was just because he liked to fight, and of course every time he had a fight, he was called into old man Goslin's office. Goslin, the high school principal, didn't like fighting.

Al had been in love with Janice Hart all year. No, love wasn't the word. It wasn't in his vocabulary, and he had never experienced the emotion to his knowledge. In any case, Janice was in his thoughts most of his waking hours, he dreamed about her at night, and he felt a warm glow if he had a chance to exchange a few words with her at school.

Now it was June and school was almost out, but he hadn't really done anything about letting Janice know how he felt. She was a year younger than he was, a sophomore, a pretty, graceful girl who was, even at her age, the most mature girl in school. Physically she was a woman, so much so that it excited him to see her walk down the hall ahead of him.

He hadn't asked her for a date because he didn't think he had any chance with her. She belonged to one of Royal's better families, her father having the biggest store in town, whereas Al lived with his widowed mother at the edge of Royal in a sod house. His mother took in washing and did ironing and housekeeping, and anything else she could to make a little money, and Al did odd jobs during the school year and worked on farms near Royal in the summer. Together they made out and that was about all.

Another thing was that Janice went steady with Ronnie Purvis, the only son of Royal's Number One family. Ronnie's father was the banker. Socially, maybe, Janice and Ronnie made a pretty good pair, Al thought, but they didn't match up any other way that he could see. None of the boys liked Ronnie, and for the life of him, Al couldn't guess what Janice saw in a skinny, sneaky, smart-aleck bastard like Ronnie Purvis.

The more he thought about it, the more Al was convinced that Ronnie was doing exactly what Janice wanted done, that they weren't just talking about their Latin or the weather in Gillette's barn. Al hadn't exactly spied on them, but he knew where they went at least three evenings a week, and had been going ever since the weather had warmed up enough for them to be out. To Al it added up to just one certain fact, that Janice's record of not having missed Sunday School for five years didn't mean a damned thing.

So, on Monday afternoon of the last week of school, Al waited for her on the corner. When she reached him, he said, "I'll walk home with you."

She hesitated, looking at him questioningly. He didn't know what she was thinking, unless she was worried that Ronnie Purvis might object. Finally she said, "All right, Al."

"I'll carry your books," he said, and reached for them.

Again she hesitated, then she said, a little reluctantly, he thought, "All right."

He knew her pretty well. They'd been to church and school parties together, and he had one class with her, sophomore English that he'd flunked the year before. But now that he was walking beside her, he couldn't think of anything to say, and suddenly he was aware that they had covered two of the three blocks to her home and he hadn't said what he wanted to say.

"Janice," he said.

She glanced sideways at him, smiling as if amused at his awkwardness. She said, "Yes, Al?"

He blurted, "I'd like to go with you, Janice. I'm a better man than Ronnie."

"I expect you are," she said, "whatever that means."

"I'll show you." The words tumbled out of his mouth. He had to talk fast because they were only half a block from her home. "Tell Ronnie to stay home tonight. I'll be in Gillette's barn when you get there."

His words wiped the smile off her mouth. She walked faster, refusing to look at him. He didn't know what to do. He did know he'd said the wrong thing. In desperation he said, "I can do anything better than Ronnie. Let me show you."

She still looked the other way. She was almost running now. They had reached the gate of the picket fence that surrounded her house. In a moment she'd be gone. Then the thought struck him that maybe she didn't know what he was talking about. He said, "You want to be . . ." He caught himself, realizing he had almost used the wrong word. Because he couldn't think of any other way to express it, he said, "You want to be screwed, don't you?"

She opened the gate and ran up the walk to the porch. He ran beside her, angry now. She had no right to be so high and mighty, pretending to be something she wasn't. He asked hotly, "Who do you think you're fooling? I know you meet Ronnie after dark in Gillette's barn. I suppose you tell your mother you're studying with Sadie Clark, but I know different."

They had reached her porch. She jerked her books away from him and slapped him hard with her right hand, then whirled around and ran up the steps, her skirt flying away from her trim ankles. He stood there a moment after she slammed the door, then he turned and walked slowly away. He'd bungled it, he thought bitterly, but he didn't know what he should have done.

He had always taken the direct way to get what he wanted; there was no trickery or slyness in him. The method he had used with Janice would have worked with a couple of other girls he knew who lived in sod houses out on the prairie beyond his mother's place. But they weren't like Janice. He should have known better, he told himself, but he hadn't, and now he'd fixed it with her.

He was unduly silent that night while he ate supper. Concerned, his mother asked, "What's wrong, Albert? Is something worrying you?"

"No Ma," he said. "You know how it is at the end of school, with exams and everything."

That seemed to satisfy her. Al finished eating, his mind on Janice. He guessed that was the way to get ahead in the world: pretend to be one thing when you're really something very different. No one else in Royal would believe the truth about Janice. Ronnie Purvis's parents, old man Goslin, the preacher, the town marshal, Janice's parents: all of them would say she was one of the best girls in town.

Ronnie Purvis was like Janice in some ways. He was a senior and would graduate this spring. He was the best student in his class, so he would be valedictorian. Next fall he planned to go to Harvard and study law. He went to church and Sunday School as often as Janice did. One Sunday morning when the preacher was sick in bed, Ronnie had actually taken the pulpit and preached. Al was in the back row that day and had to admit that Ronnie did pretty well. But he hated him. God, how he hated him.

Al wasn't sure why he hated Ronnie so much. Maybe it was because he was having Janice three times a week. Or because Ronnie had never done a day's work in his life and probably never would, but still had everything he wanted: the best clothes money could buy, the best horse and saddle, and the best house in Royal to live in.

But probably the biggest reason was that he was a fraud. He lied, he cheated on examinations, he was cruel to anyone who was weaker than he was, he was completely selfish, yet nothing marred his shiny reputation of being the best boy in town.

What made it worse, to Al, was the fact that if anything went wrong in Royal, he was responsible. Oh, some of the people made allowances. Al didn't have a father to discipline him. No one blamed his mother because she was an honest, hard-working Christian woman who had done the best she could with a wild boy. The truth was folks believed the worst of Al Cobb. Regardless of what he said about anything, it was generally agreed that he was lying.

If someone set off a dynamite blast on the Fourth of July and broke a lot of windows, Al Cobb did it. If a horse was found in old man Goslin's office the morning after Halloween, or a bunch of privies were upset, Al did it. If there was a row during a baseball game, Al started it.

Well, it had reached the place where Al knew he had to leave town or he'd wind up in jail and disgrace his mother. But he had to see Janice before he left. Tonight was as good a time as any. Chances were she'd be in Gillette's barn after dark. Al guessed he'd see to it that Ronnie didn't show up.

But Al lingered over his supper too long. Before he got up from the table, the preacher and old man Goslin arrived. Al figured he was in trouble as soon as they came in, but he didn't know what it was about. Mrs. Cobb didn't, either, but she jumped to the same conclusion Al did. She called him in from the kitchen and sat down in a rocking chair, her hands folded, her expression showing that she expected the worst.

"What's Al done now?" she asked.

The preacher looked at Goslin and Goslin looked at the preacher. Finally the preacher said, "Mrs. Hart came to see me after school tonight. She was very upset. She didn't know whether to call the marshal or not. I told her I would see Mr. Goslin and we'd talk to Albert, and then go back to her and decide."

"What did he do?" Mrs. Cobb asked.

"Janice said that she had to stay after school to make up an algebra test she had missed last week when she was sick," Goslin said. "I checked on that with her teacher and I find it is correct. I thought I should do that even though I never doubt Janice's word. Then she said that Albert had waited outside the school and had walked home with her. Just before they reached the Hart home, Albert used some obscene words. Janice took her books away from him and slapped him, and ran into the house crying. Janice is a pure and wonderful girl, Mrs. Cobb. We simply will not have this kind of thing happening to her."

"You would never doubt Janice's word, Mr. Goslin, but I assume you would doubt Albert's." Mrs. Cobb turned to the preacher. "What about you, Mr. English? You have been our minister for a long time. You know both Janice and Albert. Would you agree that Janice always told the truth and Albert always lied?"

"Well," Mr. English said, and hesitated. He repeated the word, "Well," then added, "I wouldn't go so far as to say that, but I cannot see any reason for Janice lying about this." He looked directly at Al. "Albert, did you use an obscene word to Janice?"

"No, I didn't," Al said. "I walked home with her, all right, and carried her books and she slapped me. That much is true."

"Janice isn't in the habit of going around slapping boys," the preacher said. "Why did she slap you?"

Al shrugged. "I dunno. She got mad at me, I guess. I told her I wanted a date and that I was a better man than Ronnie Purvis. That was when she got mad. Is that obscene?"

The preacher suppressed a smile and glanced at old man Goslin. "No, Albert, I wouldn't say that it was." He rose. "Well, Mr. Goslin, I think we should go back and talk to Mrs. Hart. I do believe she is making a mountain out of a molehill."

Goslin rose, too. He wasn't quite satisfied, but he didn't know what to say, either. He started toward the door, and then he turned back. He said, "Albert, you and I know how much trouble you have made in school this year, more than either your mother or Mr. English knows. It is only fair to warn you that if there are any more complaints along this line, or if you try to demonstrate that you are a better man than Ronnie Purvis, you will be dismissed from school."

He walked out. The preacher hesitated, upset by this outburst, but he didn't know how to counteract it, so he said, "Good night, Mrs. Cobb. Good night, Albert," and followed old man Goslin.

Al's mother sat there looking at him, then she began to

cry. She said, "I don't know what to do with you, Albert. I've raised you the best I could, but you keep getting into trouble. You're going to disgrace me before you're done. I just don't think I can stand it any longer."

He stared at her, feeling mean and rebellious, and wanting to hurt her. Of all people, she should understand him and love him and believe in him. He was surprised when he realized the word love had occurred to him again. It was not a word his mother ever used to him. He said, "I guess I will, Ma. I'll go out to Colorado. Looks like we'd both be better off."

"Yes, Albert," she said. "I guess we would."

He got up and left the house. She was afraid of being disgraced. That was the only thing that mattered to her. If he got into trouble in Colorado and the story never got back here, it would be all right with his mother. Her good name wouldn't be tarnished.

He walked around until dusk, trying to work things out in his mind. He'd leave in the morning. There wasn't any sense of going to school the rest of the week. He didn't have much idea where he'd go or what he'd do, but he'd worked on farms enough to know he could do anything that had to be done on farms. He was a good hand with horses, too. Maybe he could catch on with some ranch. But the main thing was to get out of Royal, to leave a home where he wasn't wanted. If he was going to see Janice again, he had to do it tonight.

First he went to the Purvis home and rang the bell. Mrs. Purvis opened the door. She stood there blinking, not recognizing him for a moment in the gathering twilight, and when she did, she backed up, frightened and shocked at his temerity.

"I want to see Ronnie," Al said.

"What about?" Mrs. Purvis asked.

"School business," Al answered.

She hesitated, not liking this. She was afraid he would contaminate Ronnie, he thought. But she finally disappeared and a moment later Ronnie came to the door, holding back a little in the hall as if not wanting to get too close to Al.

"What do you want, Cobb?" Ronnie asked. "I haven't got much time. I'm working on my valedictory. I have to give it Friday night, you know."

"Yes, I know," Al said in a low tone. "It's a good thing you've got plenty to do. I just wanted to be sure you didn't go to Gillette's barn tonight to see Janice. I'm going."

Ronnie looked as if he had received an electric shock. His face turned white and he began to tremble, but he didn't say a word. The chances were he couldn't, Al thought.

"If you stay home and work on your valedictory," Al said, "nobody's going to be hurt, but by God, if you come nosing around Gillette's barn tonight, I'll beat the living hell out of you."

Al walked off, leaving Ronnie staring at his back. If it had been anyone but Ronnie Purvis, he wouldn't have gone at it this way, but Ronnie was easily scared. This was all it would take, Al thought as he walked to Gillette's barn. Ronnie would be sore, but he'd stay away.

The barn sat on the back of the lot behind an empty

house, and hadn't been used since the Gillettes had left town the first of the year. Actually it was more of a shed than a barn, having been used by the Gillettes for their horses. There was just one door on the stable side. For some reason, the big door on the other side which was used to store hay was closed by a padlock, but the small door on the stable side was held shut only by a turn pin.

When Al arrived, he found that the turn pin had been twisted and the door wasn't closed. That was the first time he was sure Janice would be there. He stepped inside and, pulling the door shut, slipped the hook into a staple. No one could get in now, he told himself, as he stepped into a stall and climbed over a manger.

"I'm back here," Janice said.

She probably thought it was Ronnie, for it was very dark inside the barn, and he was certain she couldn't see him well enough to recognize him. Even though she was wearing a white dress, he could barely see her lying on the hay in the corner, so he was surprised when she said, "Come on, Al. You aren't scared of me, are you?"

"No," he answered. "I just thought you'd think I was Ronnie."

"Oh no," she said peevishly. "Ronnie had to work on his valedictory tonight. I'm on my way to study with Sadie, but I thought I'd stop here just to see if you were serious about your obscene proposal." She laughed softly. "I had to tell Mamma something. You should have seen her faunch around when she heard."

He dropped down beside her, thinking that if he had known how it was, he wouldn't have warned Ronnie to stay away. He realized with a sudden sense of uneasiness that it had been a mistake.

"You raised hell, too," he said glumly. "The preacher and old man Goslin came around. Goslin said he'd kick me out of school if there were any other complaints like this. He said they weren't going to have things like that happening to their good girls."

Janice giggled. "You see I *am* a good girl. Everybody thinks so but you. How did you know any different?"

"Because I knew you'd been coming here to meet Ronnie," he answered. "You wouldn't come for any other reason, would you?"

She didn't say anything for a moment, and when she did, she ignored his question. She said, "If you've guessed it, maybe other people have, too."

"Nobody would think anything like that of you," he said. "I wouldn't have if I hadn't stood outside your house and watched for you, just hoping I'd get a glimpse of you. I followed you here once and when I saw Ronnie come, I knew."

She was silent again for a moment, then she said with some bitterness, "It's too bad to have my reputation. People will be awfully shocked when they find out the kind of a girl I am. I'm not good, Al. I'm not good at all, but Mamma doesn't know it. Neither does Mr. English or Papa or old man Goslin. Sometimes I'd like to tell them the truth."

"At least people believe in you," he said bitterly, "but everybody thinks I'm no good. Even my own mother. I'm leaving home tomorrow. If I stay here, I'll disgrace Ma. She said so."

"Oh Al." She reached out and took his hand. "I don't

think what other people do about you. You're not a hypocrite like me and Ronnie and everybody else. You're honest. You don't pretend to be something you're not."

He had told himself that very thing many times, but he'd never heard it from anyone else, not even his mother. Suddenly he felt like a small boy who needed to cry. So many things were mixed up; nothing was really black or white, or good or bad.

Then he remembered what Janice had told her mother. He demanded, "Why did you tell your ma what you did? You didn't have to say that."

"Yes I did," she said. "It was what she wanted to think about you. She wouldn't have believed it if I'd said it about Ronnie. She was looking out of the window and was watching us. I knew because I saw her face at the window. That's why I slapped you. When I got inside, she asked me what happened and I told her what she expected to hear. I had to do it."

She moved close to him and, slipping an arm under his neck, brought her face close to his and kissed him. She drew her mouth away from his long enough to whisper, "Ronnie doesn't have any nerve. He just touches me. That's all he'll do." She kissed him again, then she said, "I wasn't surprised about you. I was hoping you'd think of me that way."

This time when she kissed him, she became a living fire in his arms. She whispered, "We've got to hurry or Sadie will wonder what happened to me."

He felt her tongue and her teeth; his right hand slid down along her dress to her knees, then slipped between them and she squeezed them hard against his hand. That was when they smashed the door in, the town marshal and old man Goslin and Janice's father. She sat up, screaming, "Help! Help!"

Her father leaped over the manger. The gleam from a bull's-eye lantern in the marshal's hand was fixed on Al's face. Somehow in jerking his hand back from Janice's knees in his first moment of panic, a finger caught in her skirt and tore it.

Her father was on him, hitting him with one hand and then the other, all the time yelling, "You bastard! You filthy bastard!" Goslin pulled him off, asking, "How did this happen, Janice?"

She stood on the far side of the barn, cowering against the wall, one hand holding her dress together where Al had ripped it. She was crying, but she stopped long enough to say, "I was going over to Sadie's to study. He was waiting here at the corner of the barn. When I came by, he grabbed me and dragged me inside. I couldn't get away."

They believed her. They'd have believed anything she said, he thought. He should have known. He wouldn't get a chance to leave town now. They didn't ask where she had been all this time, or why she hadn't screamed before they broke the door down. She was a good girl, so they never questioned a word she said.

The marshal took him to jail. There was some talk around town of lynching him, but nothing came of it. His mother visited him once. She cried all the time she was there and said he had disgraced her just as she knew he would.

They sent him to the reform school for three years. His

mother didn't write to him and he didn't write to her. Six months before he was released the preacher wrote that his mother had died. From a broken heart, the preacher said.

CHAPTER III

LINCOLN DREWS was no spellbinder, but he was honest and hard working, and he had done as good a job defending Al Cobb as anyone could have done. But the fact remained that he had lost the case. Cobb didn't blame him, but he blamed himself. He was the only man Cobb would talk to, the only man Cobb trusted, and the fact that Drews had grown to like his client only made him feel worse.

In a few minutes less than twenty-six hours, Al Cobb would hang. Drews had done all he could through the courts. He had called the Governor, but he had nothing new to offer in the way of evidence, so the Governor was irritated and refused to do anything. Now, with time running out, Drews didn't know what else he could do. Still, he was haunted by the feeling that there was something strange about this whole case.

His desk was covered with legal papers of one kind or another. He had a great deal to do, work that had piled up on him because he had put so much time on the Cobb case. He shoved the papers back, knowing he couldn't concentrate on anything today or tomorrow, either, until noon. Probably not then, either. He didn't know what he'd do if they hanged Cobb. He did know he'd be a sick man.

One of the odd things about the case was that he was probably the only man in Dead Horse who was sympathetic to Al Cobb. He didn't think it was due to the fact that Cobb was known to have ridden with the Wild Bunch. Cassidy and some of the others were well liked by a good many Wyoming people. In a way Drews felt that Cobb's relationship with the outlaws was an asset, and therefore had made no effort during the trial to hide it.

It was also a well-known fact that Cobb had hired out to a group of settlers in the northern part of the state as a gunfighter, and had killed several men in street brawls. Here again Drews felt that Cobb's background would not hurt him, but might even be an asset.

The murdered deputy, Lee Fawcett, was not a paragon of virtue. He had been a blusterer, a loudmouth, a man who liked to use his authority, and he had a talent for licking the hands of the important men of the community. In that way he was much like his boss, Sheriff Fred Bentley. Drews hadn't made up his mind which one was the worst. On occasion the honesty of both men had come under question, but Drews had never had the kind of evidence he had felt he could take into court.

One part of the picture which Drews still did not understand was Ronald Purvis's hatred for Cobb, which seemed to Drews to go beyond the bounds of normal human feeling and which Purvis had never explained. Another angle which puzzled Drews was the fact that Mrs. Purvis had not missed a day of the trial. He had no idea what the connection was between Mrs. Purvis and Cobb, or even if there was any. Drews assumed that the three of them had been children together in some small Nebraska town, but that had been years ago. To Drews, it made less than sense that a childhood dislike would be nurtured by Purvis until it grew into the vindictive feeling that the man obviously had for Al Cobb.

Thoughtful, Drews filled his pipe and lighted it. He rose and walked to the window that looked down into Dead Horse's Main Street. His office was over Walker's hardware store in the center of the principal business block. From here he could see Purvis's bank on the corner, the only stone building in town. Whipple's print shop was next, then the hotel, the Mercantile, and a millinery shop. On beyond the corner was a square which held the courthouse and the jail behind it. Here the scaffold had been built which would take Al Cobb's life, if Drews didn't pull a rabbit out of his hat.

Drews's pipe had gone out. He started to reach for a match when he saw Mrs. Purvis turn the corner at the bank. He assumed that she was going into the bank to see her husband, but he soon discovered he was wrong. She crossed the street at the corner, holding her skirt daintily above her ankles as she waded the dust. Damned pretty ankles they were, too, Drews told himself. In fact, Mrs. Purvis was a damned pretty woman.

Drews was a bachelor, and whenever he looked at Mrs. Purvis, he found himself entertaining thoughts that were not exactly fitting for a man of his position. He smiled, thinking that at least they made entertaining daydreams. He had a conviction that Mrs. Purvis was a woman who might have the same thoughts he did, but from the female point of view. He had decided a long time ago that she deserved a better husband than the slender, ascetic man to whom she apparently had been married for a number of years.

He relighted his pipe, reluctantly forcing his thoughts from Mrs. Purvis back to Al Cobb. The case had seemed a simple one. The Purvis's three-year-old boy had been kidnapped from his home in Dead Horse and held for $10,000 ransom. Cobb claimed he had found the boy in a deserted line cabin in the hills above town. He had heard about the kidnapping, and when the boy said his name was Jerry, Cobb jumped to the conclusion that he was the missing Purvis boy.

Cobb swore that he was bringing the child to his parents when Lee Fawcett met him in the road and started shooting. Cobb admitted he had killed the deputy, but said it was self-defense. Sheriff Fred Bentley and the prosecution contended that Cobb had kidnapped the boy, and was bringing him to town to collect the ransom, but when he saw Fawcett, he knew he was in trouble and pulled his gun.

The fact that the deputy had three spent shells in his .45 meant nothing, the prosecutor said. Cobb probably stopped, drew Fawcett's gun and fired three shots. Leaving the body beside the road, he came on to town, left the boy at the Purvis house, and was promptly arrested by Bentley when he left the Purvis place. He was charged at first with kidnapping, and later, when Fawcett's body was found, he was indicted and tried for murder.

The point that had bothered Drews the most, right from the first, was the obvious fact that kidnapping a child was a crime which did not fit a man like Al Cobb. He had hammered on the idea all through the trial, but it apparently meant nothing to Judge Charnley or the jury. Cobb was a known bad man, he admitted bringing the boy to Dead Horse, he admitted firing the shot that killed Lee Fawcett, and that was all it took to convict him.

Sheriff Fred Bentley's testimony had been damaging. He swore that the deputy always told a man he was under arrest. That made it murder, and according to Bentley it was stupid to think that Fawcett had fired three shots before Cobb killed him, that if Fawcett had actually fired the shots himself, he had done so because Cobb had not surrendered when he'd been arrested.

The prosecutor said in his summary that if Cobb's story was true, then Fawcett had tried to murder him while Cobb was carrying a three-year-old child in his arms. That was simply too ridiculous to be believed. It wasn't for Lincoln Drews, but apparently it was for the jury.

Drews heard the office door open. Turning, he saw Mrs. Purvis come in. She slid into the room quickly, almost furtively it seemed to Drews, and closed the door. Then she faced Drews, asking, "Could I talk to you for a minute?"

"Of course," he said, and motioning to a chair, sat down behind his desk.

She sat down, smoothing her skirt over her legs. Drews had a sudden desire to stand up and bend over the desk to see if her ankles were exposed, but he stifled the impulse. She was wearing a gray suit, the skirt making a tight fit across her hips. Her hat was a wide-brimmed straw with a long red plume, the tip of it reaching behind her head and quivering with each movement she made.

For a time she was silent, her head tipped forward so that the hat brim partially hid her face. Then she raised her head and he saw that her eyes were green. They were searching eyes, perhaps a little bold, but they were honest, and he thought they showed genuine concern.

Her lips were red and full, the lips of a passionate woman. His gaze dropped to her breasts that pressed firmly against her blouse. He was not a lecher, but without a word being spoken he was filled with an almost overpowering hunger for her, and a haunting feeling that she would welcome him. That, he decided quickly, was simply wishful thinking.

Quickly he turned his gaze from her, and reaching for his pipe which he had laid on the desk in front of him, he lighted it with considerable care. Again the thought came to him that this woman was being wasted on Ronald Purvis.

"I may seem impertinent," she said, "but I want to make some guesses about you. I don't really know much about you, Mr. Drews, so if I'm wrong, correct me. You are about thirty-five, single, an honest lawyer—sometimes a rare person in a small place like this—and you have a reasonably good practice in a cow-country town which is filled with dishonest pressures and influences."

He smiled around his pipe stem. "For a woman who knows very little about me, you are doing well. I'm thirty-three. On the other counts, you are correct."

She nodded. "Now, if you are able to free Al Cobb, your name would become known overnight all over

Wyoming. Colorado, too, I suppose. It would be fair to say that your name would be headlined in many newspapers. It might even open up a political career for you, and you could probably move to Cheyenne and become one of the important lawyers of the state."

He didn't know what she was driving, at, but he was irritated just the same. He had an idea she was like her husband, convinced that money would and could buy anything. He said, "Mrs. Purvis, I pride myself on being a simple man, with simple tastes which I am able to satisfy here in Dead Horse. The things you're talking about mean nothing to me."

She leaned forward, her lips parted, her gaze fixed, so directly on him that he was forced to look away. He thought angrily, *Damn such a woman. She'd make a seventy-year-old monk horny as hell just by looking at him.*

"Are you being honest, Mr. Drews?" she asked in a low tone.

He shook his head, grinning. "No, I guess I'm not. I'd like headlines. I'd like a political career. I might even like to move to Cheyenne. But you got under my hide just now. I did the best I could for Al Cobb, Mrs. Purvis. I like him and I don't think he's guilty of murder. If I knew anything I could do now, I'd do it."

"I lie, Mr. Drews," she said. "My husband lies. I'm sure the sheriff lies. The most honest man in town is Al Cobb." She sank back in her chair, her face shadowed by an expression he could not identify. Perhaps it was fear, possibly regret. Then she said slowly, "I like Al Cobb, too. If I had not liked him so well, he would not be locked up waiting to hang tomorrow. I want him saved.

If money can . . ."

"It can't," Drews said. "Why have you waited so long, Mrs. Purvis? He has about twenty-five hours. That's not enough time."

She lowered her head so that the hat brim hid her face again. "I thought I could not pay the price it may take to free him," she said. "I know now I can. I know that if I let him hang, I will pay a far bigger price than if I tell the truth." She looked up, her gaze meeting his. "Mr. Drews, I'm prepared to pay with my future, my good name, and my marriage. I'll give up anything except my son. What will it take to save Al?"

"New evidence," he said. "Important evidence that will give me a legitimate excuse to call the Governor."

"Where could we start?"

"Maybe with Fred Bentley. If we had the full truth from him, we'd have a place to work from. There's something else I need to know. Why does your husband hate Cobb so much?"

She rose, quite pale, and he wished he hadn't asked the question. If Cobb meant so much to her, she should answer the question, but he realized now that it was too embarrassing for her.

"I believe I can do something with Fred Bentley," she said. "I'll think about it. About the other. I can't tell you now. I'd rather have Al tell you. For some quixotic reason he hasn't told all he could. Perhaps he has been silent out of respect for me, but he owes me no respect. Not that much at least. I want you to go to him and tell him that. See if you can get him to talk to you. Then I want you to come to dinner at my house at noon. Ronnie is eating in the hotel dining room. There will just be you and I and Jerry."

She turned and walked out, not giving him a chance to say no. He started to call to her, but he did not. He had never been in the Purvis house. This was too good a chance to miss.

CHAPTER IV

JANICE PURVIS hurried home the way she had come, across Main Street and past the bank on the corner, and then across the bridge that spanned Dead Horse Creek. She climbed the short hill to her house. No, Ronnie's house, she told herself bitterly. Nothing that Ronnie had was hers, and that meant she had nothing except her son Jerry. Nothing! Not even Al Cobb, who would die in 25 hours from now on the scaffold they had built for him.

She opened the gate in the iron fence that circled the front yard, stepped inside, and closed the gate. For just a moment she stood staring at the big brick house in front of her: the spacious lawn which served so well for croquet on Saturday afternoons when Mr. and Mrs. Fred Bentley, or Judge and Mrs. Jacob P. Charnley, or Mr. and Mrs. Alexander H. Whipple, dropped in, as they often did, and stayed for cake and coffee.

And the deer! The massive bronze deer that Ronnie had brought from Denver the last time he was there. Janice hated it because it was something else by which Ronnie could show his affluence to the people of Dead Horse. Ronnie loved it for exactly the same reason.

She walked on up the path to the front door with its panes of colored glass around the big frosted pane in the middle. The fact that her marriage had lasted as long as it had was something of a miracle, she thought. Certainly Ronnie did not need a wife. It was different with her. She needed a husband and Ronnie was less than adequate.

These were forces which were great enough to break up any marriage, but there were contrary forces which had kept them together. At first she had thought that wealth and prestige and social position would be enough for her. Too, she'd had the vain hope that Ronnie would change. She had known him before they were married. God, how well she had known him. She should have foreseen that merely standing up before a preacher and repeating some vows would not change him. Later, after she had finally realized she could not go on this way, she had found that she was pregnant, so she had hung on for the baby's sake.

As for Ronnie, the answer was simple. He was great for show, great for convincing people that he had the best of everything. His one talent was making money. She could not deny that. When it came to giving her money for her personal use, he was so frugal he was childish, but for her clothes, for furniture, for entertainment, for help in the house, even for her horse and buggy, his largesse was unbelievable.

The truth was he needed her. She was a showcase for him like the big house, the spacious lawn, and the bronze deer. She was attractive enough to appeal to men of any age or position, so attractive that Sheriff Fred Bentley had indicated, and not very subtly, that he was her slave if she so desired. She didn't, for Bentley was gross and vulgar and foul-talking.

She hated the sheriff, but she'd never let him know how she felt. This was a game in which she had great skill, never quite closing the gate but never leaving it wide open, either. That was the way Ronnie wanted it.

She hurried along the hall to the kitchen, trying to put these things out of her mind. It was painful to remember, too painful to think of how it might have been, too painful to think of the future, for Al Cobb would die at high noon tomorrow. Lincoln Drews had made it worse with his question: "Why have you waited so long?" She had no answer that could have satisfied him, no answer that even satisfied herself.

Her housekeeper, Maggie Nolan, was busy in the pantry. Janice said, "Mr. Lincoln Drews will be here for dinner. Try to make it a little special."

"Yes, mum." Maggie looked up from her pie dough. "Will Mr. Purvis be here, too?"

"No. Just Jerry and I and Mr. Drews."

"Yes, mum. I'll do me best."

Janice smiled as she went on through the kitchen to the back yard. Maggie had a way of saying things with a sort of sniff, to indicate that she considered certain activities immoral or maybe downright sinful. Entertaining Mr. Lincoln Drews for dinner came under that category.

Jerry was playing in his sand box with Lena Walker, the girl who took care of him in the daytime, and in the evening when Janice had other obligations. If Lena had been with him the afternoon he had been kidnapped, perhaps it wouldn't have happened, but it had been late and

Ronnie was home from the bank. Lena has asked if she could get off a little early, and Ronnie had said he would look after the boy. Janice was helping Mrs. Whipple at the church and hadn't come home.

She was not even sure yet whether it had been carelessness or intent, on Ronnie's part, that had permitted the boy to wander off, but when she came home, the boy was gone. Later that night they had received the ransom note.

Jerry glanced up from the sand box, saw Janice and ran to her, his arms out. She lifted him high above her head while he kicked and squealed, then she held him close and he kissed her on the cheek and said, "I wuv you, Mamma."

"I love you, too," Janice whispered. She put him down, adding, "You play with Lena and pretty soon it will be time for dinner."

She turned and went back into the house, fighting the threatening tears. She had been that way with him ever since Al Cobb had brought him home. All Jerry had to do was to say, "I wuv you, Mamma." She could not remember ever saying that to her mother or hearing her mother say she loved her. Al said it had been the same in his home. Love was not a word that was used except in the abstract sense that God loved everybody.

Children were raised to be Spartans, she thought. They were taught honor and integrity and morals, but not the emotion of love. That was one of the things that was wrong with Ronnie, she told herself as she climbed the stairs to her room. It had been true of her, too, until she had learned to love Al Cobb, but by that time it was too late.

She took off her hat and laid it on the bureau. She looked at the clock: Eleven forty. In twenty-four hours and twenty minutes they would kill Al Cobb. She dropped face down on the bed, and because she had opened the door, she began to remember, and then, remembering, she could not close the door.

CHAPTER V

EVEN when Janice and Ronnie were small, the Harts and Purvises had more or less of an understanding with each other that when the children grew up they would marry. At least that was the way the four parents hoped it would be. The families visited back and forth on Sundays and holidays, and often in the middle of the week. Neither family made plans for a vacation without consulting the other.

It was natural and unavoidable, and certainly good in the eyes of all four parents, that the children were together a great deal. Even when Janice was five and Ronnie seven, she was the more developed of the two. In many ways she looked after Ronnie, almost mothering him. This pleased Mrs. Hart and rather astonished Mrs. Purvis, who had no other children, and was quite unaware that Ronnie was a little backward for his age.

They often went to the toilet together and examined each other with natural childish curiosity. Neither mother was aware of this, but both understood that Ronnie had a multitude of buttons, some of which he couldn't manage but which Janice could.

Both became modest as they grew older, a period that lasted several years, before they began spending their spring evenings in Gillette's barn. At first it was a sort of lark, lying together in the darkness, and shivering a little as the wind snapped at them through the cracks in the boards, and just knowing that they were alone.

Later Ronnie put his arm around her and kissed her. This wasn't enough to satisfy her, and that was why he began to touch her. She did not understand for a long time afterwards that emotionally and physically she was a woman. Ronnie was a long way from being a man even at seventeen.

Janice had been bothered all winter by the fact that she had been attracted to Al Cobb. She had known him for years, of course, but only as another boy who was a year ahead of her in school. Now that he was sixteen she became very much aware that he was good-looking, big, and possessing a virility that by contrast made Ronnie seem childish.

All through her sophomore year Al acted as if he wasn't aware that she existed, so when he waited for her that evening after school, she was more thrilled by having him walk home with her and carry her books than she would admit. Her first impulse, when he told her he would see her in Gillette's barn, was to be thoroughly angry because he knew she met Ronnie there, and because he had enough gall to think he could pick up where Ronnie left off. That was why she slapped him and ran into the house.

Her mother saw it and had to know what happened. Janice said the first thing that occurred to her—that Al had used an obscene word in her presence. She did not realize, in that first moment of panic, that her mother would have the spell about it that she did; but it was too late then. She had to stick with her story.

Later, alone in her room, she began to wonder if Al would come to the barn after dark. Ronnie wouldn't, she knew, but Al might be in trouble with the fuss her mother had raised. The more she thought about it, the more she knew she couldn't risk missing him. There was a chance he would come. She wanted to find out, she told herself, whether he was as much of a man as he had bragged.

She did not know for a long time that Ronnie was responsible for what happened. She was so ashamed of herself for putting the blame on Al, and taking the easy way out, that she had never wondered about what had brought the marshal and her father and old man Goslin to the barn. What was worse, she found herself the center of attention and that terrified her. She was afraid the truth would come out.

Her mother fainted when she found out what had happened, then she had hysterics. Janice's father had to call the doctor, and her mother finished the night by demanding that Janice be examined. She didn't believe Janice when she said nothing had happened to her.

After that she hated her mother. When she learned that her father, more than anyone else, was responsible for Al being sent to the reform school, she hated him. She didn't excuse herself. She went to the marshal and old man Goslin and tried to tell the truth; but they thought she felt sorry for Al and wouldn't believe her. She never tried to tell her father because she knew it would be useless.

They sent Al away without letting her see him, and she was sure he hated her. She didn't see much of Ronnie that summer. She stayed in her room as much as she could, wanting only to be away from everyone and everything. Late in August Ronnie came over during supper one evening, and afterwards she couldn't get rid of him. That was when he told her he was the one who had brought the men to Gillette's barn and saved her, as he put it, "from a fate worse than death."

She had never been as angry in her life as she was at that moment. He didn't understand. He had done the only thing he could, he said. She stood there hating him, her fists clenched at her sides. She told herself that if she had a gun she would kill him. She ran upstairs to her room and locked herself in, and stayed there all the following day.

The next two years were hard ones. She didn't go to parties. She refused to see Ronnie when he was home from Harvard. She wouldn't have dates with any boy. She found it hard to be civil to either of her parents. They were hurt by her attitude, and did not have the slightest notion of what caused her to treat them the way she did. She wrote letters to Al and burned them. He hated her, she thought. He'd have to. She often thought of visiting his mother but gave that up, too. Mrs. Cobb must hate her.

The third year was better because she went away to a girls' school in St. Louis. She didn't have to fight Ronnie off, or quarrel with her mother, or be coldly silent with her father. She had a few girl friends but not many. She was too attractive and most of them were jealous of her.

There were dates and boys and dances, and some of the pain and the hate went out of her. For the first time in three years she was sorry to see a school year come to an end.

When she returned home, Ronnie was waiting for her. He asked her to marry him, but she couldn't stand him. Still, he hung around the Hart house, lovesick and self-pitying and unable to understand why he was being treated the way he was. He was in the house the day Al Cobb returned to Royal.

Janice was sitting in the parlor listening to Ronnie tell her he would be the best student in next year's graduating class. She looked out of the window and saw Al turning in from the street. He was bigger than he had been when he'd left. He was wearing a cheap suit and he hadn't shaved for three or four days, so he looked as rough as a cowboy who had just ridden into town from the sand hills.

For a moment she couldn't move. She could think of nothing except that he must not hate her as she had supposed. He wouldn't be coming to see her if he did. She flung the door open and ran out of the house, leaving Ronnie in the middle of a sentence. She cried, "Al, Al," and ran into his arms.

He was too surprised to know what to do with her. She hugged him and kissed him and cried, her tears making the front of his shirt wet. She kept saying, "All this time I thought you hated me or I would have written to you." He didn't deny it. He stood on the porch just above the steps, too amazed to do anything.

Ronnie had come out of the house. When he saw what

was going on, he yelled, "Get away from her, Cobb. Haven't you done enough to her?"

Al pushed her away, grinning. "I'm glad to see you, Purvis. I've owed you something for a long time."

She cried out, "Don't, Al." Instinctively she knew how this would end.

But Al didn't listen. Ronnie swung a fist, a looping blow that Al ducked. Then Al threw a punch. He hit Ronnie on the point of the chin, knocking him over the porch railing. He struck the grass on his head and shoulders and flattened out and didn't get up.

Terrified, Janice cried, "You've killed him, Al. You've got to run."

She knelt beside Ronnie and felt for his pulse, but she couldn't find it. She rose and whirled to face him. "He's dead, Al. I'll say I did it. Go on. Run. Get out of town. You know what they'll do to you for this."

He stood there staring at her uncertainly. From inside the house her mother called, "What's going on out there, Janice?"

"You've got to run," Janice whispered fiercely. "I got you into trouble once, but I'll get you out of this. I told you I'd say I did it. They'll believe me. I've been fighting with him for three years."

He ran, then, around the house, as Mrs. Hart came out to see what had happened. Ronnie wasn't as dead as Janice had thought, but he was badly hurt and he didn't regain consciousness for several hours. By the time he did and told what had happened, Al had jumped a freight train and was miles out of town.

Ronnie and her folks were furious with her because

she had lied to protect Al. She didn't defend herself. She let them talk, thinking that sooner or later she would hear from Al. But the months passed and she didn't.

That winter her mother died. When Ronnie returned to Royal after being graduated with honors, he put out his shingle and started practicing. She agreed to marry him. It would be better, she thought listlessly, than keeping house for her father.

If Al had sent for her, she would have gone to him. Anywhere and any time. But he didn't. She could well understand that he was glad to be away from her and Ronnie and her father, and everyone else in Royal.

She married Ronnie early that fall and they went to Niagara Falls. The honeymoon was exactly what she had expected it to be.

CHAPTER VI

LINCOLN DREWS stood at his office window staring into the street. He watched Mrs. Purvis until she disappeared around the corner of the bank, thinking that this was the damnedest situation he had ever run into. Why would a woman in her position, married to the wealthiest and the most important man in Dead Horse, commit herself to the cause of a man like Al Cobb?

The whole business simply didn't make sense any way Drews looked at it. He repeated aloud what she had said: "Mr. Drews, I'm prepared to pay with my future, my good name, and my marriage. I'll give up anything, except my son." That was a hell of a price to pay for a man like Al Cobb, who probably didn't deserve it. Why?

He stood there a good five minutes turning this over in his mind. Did it have some connection with Ronald Purvis's abnormal hatred of Al Cobb? Was it possible that Janice Purvis was in love with Cobb? Ridiculous, he decided. Yet her visit and the things she had said were so extraordinary that he had a weird sense of having dreamed the whole thing.

He slipped his pipe and tobacco into his pocket, put on his hat, and left the office. He had talked to Cobb many times, trying to get the whole truth, but he had failed. He was convinced he was wasting his time now, but he felt he had to try again because Mrs. Purvis had asked him to.

First he would see Alex Whipple. There were many things about Whipple he didn't like. The man had a vitriolic pen and he was inclined to put expediency above principle. The part Drews disliked the most was his attack upon Cobb and his quoting Purvis, but it was easy to guess the reason. Cobb had been found guilty of murder, he was to be hated, so Whipple was merely giving the people what they wanted to read.

Purvis had followed the same line, but it plainly had been personal with him. It hadn't been with Whipple. He'd go with the wind, particularly if the wind blew in a direction which favored him. Above all things he was ambitious, and if Drews could fan that ambition, he'd have the man bought and delivered. He would keep his word. That, as far as Drews knew, was the one characteristic in Whipple which was admirable.

Drews crossed the street to Whipple's print shop and

found him chewing hard on a cold cigar, his pen clutched in his right hand, a stack of paper in front of him covered by his handwriting.

"Looks as if you're writing the great American novel," Drews said.

"Long enough to be a novel," Whipple said. "No, I'm doing what will eventually be a series of articles on the irrigation project that Purvis is pushing. He's putting up most of the money, but he says he can't swing all of it. I promised to help promote it."

Drews groaned. This would make it tougher to pull Whipple to his side.

"What's the matter with you?" Whipple demanded. "You against it?"

"Sure I am," Drews said, "unless Purvis puts up all the money. Whenever he invites other people to invest in one of his ideas, he's got an angle."

Whipple laughed. "Sure he has, but if it benefits Dead Horse, why should we kick?"

"Yeah, if it does," Drews said. "Come on. You're working too hard. I'll buy you a drink."

Whipple jumped up with alacrity and took his derby off a nail in the wall. "I'd be a fool to turn that down. If Linc Drews, the well-known tightwad, offers to buy a drink for a poor editor, it comes under the heading of a miracle. Besides, you've got an angle yourself and I'm curious about what it is."

"The well-known tightwad," Drews said as they stepped into the street. "I resent that, suh."

"Pistols at sunrise," Whipple said, laughing. He glanced sideways at the lawyer as they crossed the street.

He was five feet five inches tall. Drews was six feet three inches, so Whipple had to tip his head to see the lawyer's face. "If you'd grow a beard, you'd sure look like old Abe."

"I look like young Abe," Drews said. "Before he grew a beard."

"That why your mother named you Lincoln?"

"That's right," Drews said with great gravity. "I distinctly remember when I was born, my mother took one look at me and asked what have you delivered from my womb and the doctor said this baby is the spit'n image of Abraham Lincoln. So my mother laid back and said we will call him Lincoln."

Whipple sighed as they pushed through the batwings of the Stockman's Bar. "And they say editors are born liars."

Drews picked up a bottle and two glasses, and led the way to a back table where they wouldn't be overheard. He filled the glasses and set the bottle down. He said, "You're right, Alex. I've got an angle. How would you like to help me save Al Cobb?"

Whipple had his glass halfway to his mouth when Drews said that. He carefully put it back. He said, "Linc, if you had said that one second later when I was drinking, I'd have choked to death. My God, man, have you lost your mind? He's a dead man."

"No, we've still got more than 24 hours." Drews put his elbows on the table and leaned forward. "Listen to me, Alex. How would you like to have your name as a newspaper man known all over Wyoming, perhaps all over the Rocky Mountain region? How would you like

43

to be offered a job on a Cheyenne or Laramie news-paper? Maybe a Denver one? Or how would you like to step up your political career from Cheyenne to Washington, and be called Congressman Whipple?"

This time Whipple got his drink down. He wiped his mouth, then he asked quietly, "Where do you buy your pipe tobacco, Linc? You know, they're putting something into it besides tobacco."

Drews shook his head. "I'm dead serious, Alex. For one thing, you sure don't owe Ronald Purvis anything. I hear he's talking of running against you in the next election."

"Yeah, I heard the same," Whipple muttered. "The son of a bitch."

"The party needs money," Drews said. "Purvis will make a big contribution."

"What the hell are you getting at?" Whipple asked uneasily.

"Why does Purvis hate Cobb so bad?"

"I don't know," Whipple said. "I tried to get it out of him, but I didn't. He gave me his statement like he'd thought it out word by word, and then he shut up."

"All right, I'll tell you what I'm getting at," Drews said. "The only way I can save Cobb is to get new evidence I can tell the Governor about so he'll give us a stay of execution. You and I belong to the right party and we've both been of some help to the Governor. If we work on it together, maybe we can get him to listen no matter what Purvis does. As far as you're concerned, you'd have a story that would set you up in a big way. It would help me, too."

Whipple shook his head. "It's no use, Linc. We don't have enough time. Besides, I don't care anything about Cobb. Let him swing."

Drews leaned back in his chair. "Let's see. In that long story you wrote right after Cobb was found guilty, you said he was a horse thief, a stage robber, a cattle rustler, a bank robber and a murderer. Did you have any proof for any of those accusations?"

"Hell, no," Whipple snapped, "but everybody knows he rode with the Wild Bunch. You think he was any better than the rest of them?"

"Maybe," Drews said, "maybe not. But the fact remains that you found him guilty because of his associations, not his own acts."

The editor shrugged. "Look, Linc. You defended the bastard. I guess you like him. I understand that, but I've got no reason to put myself out for him."

"Except that it might do you a hell of a lot of good," Drews said. "I've been convinced right from the first that there was something damned smelly about the whole deal. For one thing, in that same column you talked about 'our own beloved Deputy Sheriff Lee Fawcett.' Tell me who loved him, except maybe Fred Bentley."

"All right, so he was a son of a bitch," Whipple said uneasily, "but he was a law man and Cobb admitted he shot him."

"I know," Drews said. "Alex, I'm going to tell you why I'm starting to work again on what I had considered a lost cause. But you'll have to give me your word that it won't go any farther."

"Sure," Whipple said. "It must be something pretty good."

"It is. It's so good that I'vc been wondering if it really happened. It's why it will make a hell of a big story for you, but I'll make you a promise now. If you let this slip to anyone, I'll break your neck. By God, Alex, that's a promise."

Whipple looked at Drews's big hands that were spread palm down on the green-topped table, and then looked up at the lawyer's face. He said, "You know, Linc, I kind of believe you'd do it."

Drews's grin was brief and tight. "All right then, I guess we understand each other. Here it is. Mrs. Purvis came into my office this morning. She wants to help free Cobb. As near as I can remember what she said, it was this. 'I'm prepared to pay with my future, my good name, and my marriage. I'll give up anything except my son.' "

Whipple's eyes had suddenly turned bright and sharp. "Well now," he said softly, "maybe we do have a story. What are you going to do?"

"She wanted to know where to start, and I said I thought Fred Bentley had lied on the stand. I said I also wanted to know why her husband hated Cobb so much. She said she thought she could do something with Bentley, but she wanted Cobb to tell me about Purvis. I'm going to see him right now, then I'm having dinner with her and the boy in her house."

"Well," Whipple said, "I guess she could get anything out of any man except her husband. He's one cold fish. Now what do you want me to do?"

"I'll see you after I get back from having dinner with her. But I don't expect to get anything out of Cobb. I thought you might try Purvis again, maybe use that irrigation project as an excuse for going to see him. All three of them knew each other when they were kids. I think the trouble goes back to those days. I'd like to know what it is."

"I'll try," Whipple said, and held out his hand. "You know, Linc, your idea of me going to Congress sounds pretty damned good."

CHAPTER VII

A L COBB, lying on his bunk with his eyes closed, heard the heavy metal door between the sheriff's office and the cell block swing open; he heard the familiar sound of Fred Bentley's heavy steps move toward him along the corridor; then the sheriff said, "It's a quarter to twelve. Twenty-four hours from now I'll be unlocking your cell and taking you out of here. I reckon we can get to the rope that's waiting for you in fifteen minutes."

Cobb didn't open his eyes. The sheriff's round face with its heavy jowls and little, red-flecked eyes was all too familiar to him. So, too, was the smug expression of superiority, the satisfied expression of a man who has been given the right by the state to take the life of another man.

Cobb didn't see any sense in talking back to the sheriff, so he remained silent. Bentley was the kind who liked to stick a knife into a man and twist it. That was one of the first things Cobb had learned about him. He had learned, too, that he only made it worse if he responded to the sheriff's goading.

When Cobb didn't say anything, Bentley went on, "So you ain't in a talkative mood this morning. All right, you don't have to be friendly if you don't want to. I just came back to ask you what you wanted for supper. The condemned man is supposed to have anything he wants to eat before the hanging. If you think of any little tidbit that'll tickle your appetite, I'll tell old Mose in the restaurant when I go over to get your dinner."

Still Cobb said nothing. He didn't believe Bentley would tell old Mose if he asked for something special, and judging from the food he'd been getting, he didn't think old Mose could cook it so it was fit to eat if Bentley did tell him. He hadn't eaten a decent meal since he'd been in jail. For breakfast every morning he'd had two fried eggs, the yolks staring at him from the runny whites like orange pupils in a pair of rheumy eyes, two strips of fat bacon only half cooked, and coffee that tasted as if it had been made three days before and warmed up until it was strong enough to take the hide off the inside of a man's mouth. Dinners and suppers never varied: soggy potatoes, overdone steaks, dried-out biscuits, and more of the warmed-up coffee.

Bentley opened his mouth to say something when he heard his name called from the office. He swore and stomped back down the corridor. Cobb thought about the poor food he'd been given to eat since he'd been here, and how long it had been since he'd had a decent meal. He deserved one. Certainly it was a small enough favor to do for a man they were going to hang at high noon tomorrow. There wasn't any use to tell Bentley, though. If he could see Lincoln Drews . . . but there was little chance of that. The lawyer hadn't visited him for several days. Not that he blamed Drews. The man had done all anyone could do.

Cobb heard the metal door open again, heard steps, then the lock of his cell door turned and Bentley said, "You've got company, Killer."

Cobb sat up as Lincoln Drews stepped into the cell. Drews asked, "How are you, Al?"

Cobb rubbed his eyes. "For a minute I figured I was dreaming, Linc. I'd just been thinking about you. It's good to see a man once in a while. I sure get a bellyful of looking at that big ape standing behind you."

"Ape?" Bentley yelled angrily. "You'd best keep a civil tongue in your head, you God-damned killing son of a . . ."

"All right, Fred," Drews said. "Go fetch his dinner. I won't be here long."

Sullenly Bentley stepped back, closed and locked the cell door, then strode along the corridor to his office. Drews sat down on the bunk beside Cobb. He said, "You don't do yourself any good by hoorawing Bentley."

"I don't do myself no harm, neither," Cobb said. "I sure can't make things any worse."

"Maybe not." Drews lifted a handful of cigars from his coat pocket and handed them to Cobb. "I just bought these in the Stockman's Bar. I think they're reasonably fresh."

"Thanks," Cobb said gratefully. He put one in his

49

mouth, bit off the end, and lighted it, then he asked, "Could you get me a decent meal tonight? Maybe from the hotel dining room. I get damned tired of the slop Bentley keeps fetching me."

"I'll see to it," Drews promised. "Al, I have only a few minutes. I don't want to get your hopes up, but I'm still working for you. Maybe there isn't any chance, but I'm trying. Anyhow, I want you to tell me exactly what happened."

"Oh, for God's sake," Cobb groaned. "I've gone over it with you a dozen times. I told it on the witness stand. There's nothing else to tell."

"I want to hear it again."

Cobb stared at the lawyer's rugged face. No beauty, this Lincoln Drews, but an honest man if there was such a thing. He was making no promises now, and it seemed to Cobb that it was a cruel thing to have his hopes raised when there wasn't any chance of beating the rope. The deck had been stacked against him the day the trial started. Still, Drews wouldn't be here unless there was some kind of a chance.

Cobb shrugged. "All right, I'll tell it again."

"Don't leave out anything," Drews cautioned.

"I was coming up from Rawlins," Cobb said. "Just riding through the country. I'd run into a search party in the hills south of here, so I knowed about the Purvis boy being kidnapped. Bentley was running the outfit, and I've never figured out how even a stupid bastard like Bentley could have overlooked the line cabin where I found the boy, unless he had his reasons for not wanting to find him."

Drews nodded. "I've thought of that, Al, but I can't add it up and make any sense out of it."

"Me, neither," Cobb said. "Well, the trail I was on led past this cabin. I didn't know how close I was to town, and I was hungry. I stopped and tried the door, figuring I'd cook me some grub if there was anything in the cabin to eat, but the door was padlocked. I guess the kid heard me. Anyhow, he started to cry. I busted the door in, and as soon as I saw the boy, I figured he was Jerry. He was scared of me at first, but I finally got him to talking and he said that's who he was. There wasn't any grub in the cabin, but plenty of empty cans around showing it had been lived in mighty recent.

"I told the boy I'd take him home. I wasn't more'n half a mile from town when I ran into Lee Fawcett heading up the trail toward the cabin. He didn't say howdy nor nothing. He just pulled his gun and started shooting. If he'd been any good with an iron, he'd have drilled me. Maybe the kid, too, but he missed three times. Then I had my gun out and I plugged him in the brisket. I left him lying there, figuring maybe I was in trouble, but I had to take the boy to town. I done so, and right off ran into Bentley who had got back with the search party he'd been out with.

"Bentley arrested me for kidnapping the boy. Said all the evidence he needed was the fact that I'd fetched the boy in, and my story of finding him close to town in that line cabin didn't make no sense. Well, you know the rest. Jerry said I didn't take him, but nobody believed a three-year-old boy."

"Except me and his mother," Drews said. "This adds

up to about what you've said before. You're still leaving something out."

"I told you I'd said all there was to say. You want me to make up something?"

Drews shook his head. "No, Al, but I have a hunch there's something important you've been leaving out. I've got to find new evidence that you're innocent, conclusive evidence, if we're to have any chance of talking the Governor into giving us a stay of execution. Where am I going to get it if you don't give it to me?"

"What makes you so damned sure I'm holding out on you?" Cobb demanded.

"Mrs. Purvis came to see me this morning. She said you haven't told as much as you should and could."

Cobb stared at the floor. For a moment he had trouble with his breathing. Janice had stayed out of it all this time. Why couldn't she stay out of it now that there were only twenty-four hours left?

"Do you want to die?" Drews asked softly. "Is that why you insist on holding something back?"

Cobb lifted his head to stare truculently at Drews. "No, by God. I don't want to die at the end of a rope any more than the next man. There just ain't nothing more to tell about me and the boy and Lee Fawcett."

"Mrs. Purvis said she liked you. She said you were the most honest man in town." Drews paused, his gaze fixed on Cobb's face. "She said that if she hadn't liked you so well, you wouldn't be waiting to hang tomorrow. She said she wanted you saved."

Cobb jerked the half-smoked cigar from his mouth and threw it across the cell. "By God, Linc," he said furiously. "Can't you understand there's nothing else for me to tell that's got anything to do with Fawcett's killing?"

"No, I sure can't," Drews said. "I asked Mrs. Purvis why she had waited so long, and she said she'd thought she couldn't pay the price it would take to free you, but she can now. She said she was prepared to pay with her future, her good name, and her marriage, and she told me to talk to you again. I'm having dinner with her in a few minutes, and I'm supposed to tell her what you've said."

For a moment Cobb was too choked up to say anything. He stared at the floor again, old and poignant memories crowding into his mind, memories he had not wanted to remember because they were so painful. "Nothing I can say now would do any good, Linc," he muttered. "You know it as well as I do."

"No, I don't know it," Drews said. "That's why I'm here."

"All right, all right." Cobb looked up briefly, then stared at the floor again. "We grew up in the same town, me 'n Janice and Ronnie Purvis. We went to high school together, Ronnie and me both liked her. I got into trouble and they sent me to reform school. When I got out, I went back to see her. Ronnie was in the house. Janice kissed me like she was glad to see me. Ronnie came out of the house and tried to hit me. I knocked him over the porch railing and he landed on his head and shoulders. Janice thought he was dead. She said for me to run and she'd say she done it. I ran. I ain't proud of it, but I knew what they'd do to me, coming back from reform school and killing the banker's son." He leaned back against the wall, staring at Drews. "Now you know. You crazy enough to think that'll help me beat the rope?"

"No, I don't," Drews admitted. "You're sure that's all?"

"Sure it's all," Cobb said heavily. "Now get out and let me alone. I've just got twenty-four hours left. I've got a right to live it in peace."

"Yes, I guess you have." Drews rose and stood looking down at Cobb, frowning as if debating with himself whether to say anything more or not. Then he said slowly, "I'm still not satisfied that I've heard it all. Janice Purvis said that perhaps you were keeping silent out of respect for her, but that you didn't owe her that much respect."

"No, I don't," Cobb said furiously. "I sure as hell don't. Now will you get out of here and let me alone?"

"All right, Al," Drews said mildly and, turning to the door, called, "Fred."

Bentley came immediately carrying a plate of food. When he unlocked the door, Cobb yelled, "Take that swill back. I don't want it."

"It's all there is," Bentley said smugly, as Drews stepped out of the cell.

"You give it to me and I'll give it back." Cobb got up and walked to the door. "Right in your ugly mug."

Bentley retreated hastily and locked the cell door. "All right, Killer, you can go hungry. What did you do to him, Linc? I always said he was a bad one. You sure brought his meanness out."

Drews walked down the corridor and through the door, saying nothing. Bentley hesitated, holding the tin plate in front of him, then he followed the lawyer.

Cobb swung around and sat down on the bunk. He shouldn't have talked that way to Drews, he told himself with regret. Drews was honestly trying to help him. But there wasn't any hope for him now, even if he had told the rest of it. Drews must know that as well as he did. The rope was his destiny. He guessed he'd known it for a long time.

He lay down on the bunk, his eyes closed again. There was so much to remember: Janice's kiss, Ronnie Purvis's futile blow, the punch he had given Ronnie, and the wild panic that had gripped him when Janice had knelt beside Ronnie and said he was dead and for Al to run. And most of all, he remembered how certain he had been afterwards that Janice had lied to save herself and Ronnie, just as she had three years before in the barn.

CHAPTER VIII

AL COBB was sweating an hour after the freight train left Royal. He crouched in a corner of the gondola, his shirt stuck to his back between his shoulder blades. He had stopped trembling, but he had trouble breathing. His throat felt as if a noose had been tightened around his neck. That's exactly what would happen if they ever caught him and took him back to Royal for trial. They had sent him to the reform school for three years for something which had never really happened, so they'd certainly hang him for killing Ronnie Purvis.

An hour became two and then three, and as the miles increased between him and Royal, some of the terror left him. Maybe he was out of their reach now. He might even be across the state line into Colorado. And then there was a chance that Ronnie wasn't really dead. If that was true, Janice had lied to get him out of town, just as she had lied three years ago in Gillette's barn to save her own skin. This idea brought confusion to this thinking. He hoped it wasn't true.

He wasn't sure why he had gone back to Royal to see Janice. Maybe it was just to look at the town where he had been raised, as much of a home as he had ever known. Maybe to visit his mother's grave. He had intended to stay only an hour or so, and then head west for Colorado where he'd get work on a cattle ranch. But maybe, and he guessed this was the truth of it, he only wanted to see Janice again before he left for good.

She said she'd thought he hated her. Well, he had. He had reason to. Every minute he'd spent in that hell hole they called a reform school had been torture. It should have been called a deform school. Janice Hart was responsible for every second he'd spent in the place. And yet for some unexplained reason he had wanted to see her. It didn't make much sense, he told himself, that he would go back to Royal to see a girl he hated, but it was the truth.

She was pretty, prettier even than he remembered because she had matured. She'd be eighteen now, he guessed. Ronnie Purvis had been in the house, but they weren't married or she wouldn't have greeted him the way she had. One thing was sure. He wouldn't forget the way she had kissed him or how she'd cried, her tears leaving wet spots on the front of his shirt. And he wouldn't forget the wonderful satisfaction he'd had connecting with Ronnie's chin.

Al had fought and whipped most of the boys in Royal, but he'd never tangled with Ronnie before. He'd wanted to, all right, but Ronnie never fought anyone. Not with his fists anyhow. Al guessed that the other boys were just as familiar with one certain fact of life as he was, that it wasn't healthy to do bodily harm to the son of Banker Purvis.

Probably Ronnie's futile effort to hit Al was the first time in his life he'd ever thrown a blow in anger. If he hadn't, Al wouldn't have hit him no matter how much he wanted to. Now he'd killed him. He felt a chill ravel down his spine, the rope tightening around his neck again, the sweat breaking through his skin.

He could see Janice kneeling beside the motionless Ronnie and trying to find his pulse, then getting up and facing him; he could hear her cry out in a voice so high it almost broke, "He's dead, Al. I'll say I did it. Go on. Run. Get out of town. You know what they'll do to you for this." He had run because he had known exactly what they would do, and now he'd keep running, he thought, as long as he lived.

At dusk the train slowed to a crawl. Al heard a man running on the cinders beside the track. A moment later the fellow climbed over the edge and dropped into the gondola beside Al. He was startled to find someone else in the car, then his long mouth curled into a grin. "Howdy, friend," he said. "I didn't know this hotel room was occupied, but I reckon it's big enough for two."

"Sure," Al said. "Pull up a chair and be comfortable."

The grin on the long mouth widened. "Well now, I like a sense of humor in a man. It sure enough takes a sense of humor to put a chair in one of these dad-blamed Pullmans." He held out his hand. "I'm Texas Slim."

"Al Cobb."

"I had a real name like that once," the stranger said, "but I had to keep changing it. Now I disremember what it was. It gets kind of embarrassing to have to keep looking at your hatband to see what your name is, so I just call myself Texas Slim and let it go at that."

He drew makings from his pocket and rolled a smoke, his gray eyes making a frank appraisal of Al, who stared back making his own appraisal. Texas Slim was about 25, Al judged, very tall and slender, fried down to hide and bone, with the sun-blackened face and the squinting expression of a man who has spent most of his waking hours out-of-doors. He wore a weather-beaten Stetson, worn cowboy boots, and a gun belt with a walnut-handled .45 in the holster. When Al finished looking, he still couldn't figure the man out. He should be on a horse, not stealing a ride on a freight train.

"Going far, Al?" Slim asked.

"Dunno."

Slim grinned. "I don't, neither, but I've got a hunch it won't be far on this train. The damned conductor will come along purty soon and boost us off. We'd best beat him to it 'bout the time we hit Julesburg."

"How far?"

"Oh, mebbe another hour." Slim blew a lungful of smoke out through his nose, then took the cigarette from his mouth and inspected the ash. "Sure funny how old lady luck screws a man. I had a good enough job out of Ogallala a piece, but I couldn't leave the cards alone. Poker hits me like whisky or women do some men. I wound up losing my dinero, then my horse and saddle. It's a wonder I had sense enough to fold before I lost my gun. No use going back to work without a horse and saddle, so I jumped a freight, got kicked off, and then climbed in with you." He flipped his cigarette away and glanced sideways at Al. "You ain't no hobo, friend."

"No," Al agreed. "I ain't."

After a moment's silence, Slim said, "Well, I'll tell you, Al. I'm hungry. We'll get off at Julesburg and rustle something to eat."

"I'm broke."

Slim laughed. "So am I, friend, but that's no excuse for going hungry. We'll find a chicken pen with some fat old hens and we'll go down to the river and cook our supper. Then maybe if we're lucky we'll hook onto a couple of horses that nobody wants as bad as we do, and we'll get to hell out of here." He stretched and yawned. "Quite a spell yet till winter, but when snow flies, I figure to be in Brown's Hole. Ever been there?"

"No."

"It's a healthy place to spend the winter. Climate's purty good. Fine people live there who don't favor no law men snooping around. That's why some of the Wild Bunch hole up there till spring." He glanced at Al, then shrugged. "Of course it's a damned big, free country out here. You can go where you want to unless the law's on your tail, then it ain't so free."

He'd made a good guess, Al thought. Why not go

along with Texas Slim, Al asked himself? He had a lot to learn, and Texas Slim had the look of a man who knew what to teach. Al hadn't done anything criminal in his life, but he had the name. He'd gone to the reform school for something he hadn't done. Now if they caught him they'd hang him for a killing that had been an accident. Ronnie Purvis had tried to hit him and he'd hit him back, and for that they'd stretch his neck.

"Fellers like Butch Cassidy have got the right notion," Slim went on. "Used to be a cow hand, Butch did, but he's like me. He just got tired of pounding his butt against leather for thirty a month and found. He hires out on a ranch now and then, I guess, when he wants to lay low, but all the time he's planning the next job, and when he pulls it off, it pays big. Banks and trains. Hell, they've got it and they can afford to lose it. He never takes nothing from them that can't afford it, and that's being smart."

"Yeah," Al agreed, thinking he'd like to go back to Royal and take a few dollars away from Ronnie Purvis's father, maybe a few thousand. He could afford to lose it. "I guess that *is* being smart."

So he threw in with Texas Slim. There was never any pact or agreement. They simply went on together, Texas Slim the teacher, Al Cobb the pupil who realized he had a lot to learn. They stole two horses in Julesburg and lit out for the empty land to the west. Three nights later they broke into a country store south of Cheyenne and took all the money they could find, two sacks of grub, guns and ammunition. They rode on to Virginia Dale, then turned north along the edge of the mountains to Laramie.

Quite by accident, in Laramie Al learned about Ronnie Purvis. He was eating with Texas Slim at the free-lunch counter in a saloon when he saw a copy of the Denver Post. He thumbed through it, saw a headline about Royal, and read that Ronald Purvis, one of the town's most promising young men and the son of one of Royal's most eminent citizens, had been set upon and badly beaten by a thug named Al Cobb, who had just been released from the reform school. Young Purvis had been badly injured, but he was now recovering at home. Al Cobb was wanted for assault and battery.

Al tossed the paper down. He said, "Let's ride, Slim."

From the moment they'd got off the train at Julesburg, Slim had called the turns. Now he took one look at Al's face and nodded. "All right," he said. "We'll ride."

That night, crouched beside a small campfire on the Laramie Plains, Al told Slim what had happened. "I figured it was something like that," Slim said. "So you ain't wanted for murder, but you can still be in a hell of a fix. It ain't so much what you done as who you done it to, and you sure picked the wrong one to do it to. We'd best find us a job and lie low for a spell, then come fall we'll mosey into Brown's Hole."

They drifted south into North Park and found riding jobs. Later they rode on west into Steamboat Springs, and down the Yampa to Craig and into Brown's Hole. Here, for the first time in his life, Al found men he liked, men who accepted him, no questions asked. He met Butch Cassidy and Elza Lay. On several occasions, he rode with some of the bunch into Rock Springs or Baggs, where they drank too much and got into brawls.

Once he wound up in jail with Texas Slim and another man named Red Mike.

Al had his name in the newspaper. That worried him, although it was hardly likely that anyone back in Royal, Nebraska, ever saw a Rock Springs, Wyoming, newspaper. But an editor named Alexander H. Whipple, who edited the Dead Horse *Weekly Bugle*, printed the story along with an editorial appealing to the governors of Wyoming, Colorado and Utah to clean out the desperado nest in Brown's Hole, so the surrounding towns would be free from such hell raising.

In the spring when the weather cleared, the Wild Bunch moved out of the Hole, but before they did, Cassidy called Al aside. He said, "This ain't none of my business, but I'm asking anyway. You wanted by the law?"

Al grinned and nodded. "For assault and battery in Nebraska."

Cassidy said, "Oh hell! Is that all?"

"As far as I know."

"I ain't a man to give advice when it ain't asked for," Cassidy said, "but I'm offering you some. Slim ain't one to listen, but maybe you will. Don't get the law hounds on your tail. The day's gone when a man can walk into a bank and hold it up, and ride out of town without getting shot all to hell. News travels too fast with telegraph wires strung all over the country."

That was all Cassidy said, and at the moment Al didn't know exactly what he was getting at; but he knew a week later when he rode into Vernal, Utah, with Texas Slim and Red Mike. Slim started talking about a scheme he had for holding up the Vernal bank, a scheme that included all three of them.

Al cut him off immediately with a sharp no. He was riding on and getting a job. Slim cursed him bitterly, asking why Al supposed he'd picked him up in the first place and nursed him along all this time. Al said he didn't know and didn't particularly care. All he knew was that holding up the Vernal bank was a suicide notion, and Slim would get his tail shot off if he tried it.

Al kept on riding, but Texas Slim and Red Mike had to have a try at a bank south of Vernal, one small enough for the two of them to handle. A few days later Al saw their pictures in a Salt Lake City newspaper. They'd been shot to death in the street, then propped up against the front wall of the bank they'd tried to rob and their pictures taken, a dozen bullet holes in each of them.

The chances were, Al thought, that he'd have been in the picture right beside Texas Slim and Red Mike, if Cassidy hadn't talked to him the way he had. The day of the Wild Bunch was over, and no one knew it better than Cassidy himself. Al often wondered what happened to Cassidy, but he never knew for sure.

The next years were rootless ones. Al worked at a dozen things in a dozen places. He buckarooed for the Big P ranch in southeastern Oregon, he bucked logs in a logging camp in Washington, he prospected in Alaska, he carried a marshal's star in tough Nevada mining camps. He made good money, but he never saved it. He had women of all ages and sizes and dispositions and passions, but none held any lasting appeal for him. Professionals or amateurs, he walked off and forgot them five minutes after he was done with them.

The truth was, and he admitted it to himself when he was lonely enough, or drunk enough but not too drunk, that the only woman who had ever appealed to him was Janice Hart. He hated her. Sure he hated her, hated her for what she had done to him when they were kids in Gillette's barn, hated her even more for what she had done to him in front of her house in Royal, lying about Ronnie being killed and telling him to run and save his hide, when all the time she was trying to keep him from stomping the life out of Ronnie Purvis.

By now Janice was probably married to Ronnie, and they had a bunch of kids and lived in the finest house in Royal, and she had all the silk dresses a woman could want. But he loved her, too, at least he wanted her as he had never wanted another woman.

No matter how much he tried to forget her, the memory of her, the mental picture of her, clung in his mind and infuriated him. His feeling was different for Ronnie Purvis. He simply hated him. Someday he'd find the bastard and kill him. Or do something worse. He wasn't sure what that would be, but he'd think of it when the time came.

Eventually he drifted back to Brown's Hole. It was early in spring, almost exactly eight years from the time he'd left with Texas Slim and Red Mike. As was the case with so many things he did, he wasn't exactly sure why he came back, except that he didn't have any place to go, nothing else to do. He wanted to see if anyone still lived there that he knew, he told himself, but the truth was the winter he had spent in the Hole had been the happiest winter of his life. Eight years of restless wandering had done nothing for him. He had a secret hope, which was never fully articulated in his thoughts, that he would find that same happiness again.

In a way he succeeded. Many of the ranchers he remembered were still there and they remembered him. He was welcome in any of their homes. They liked to hear him tell about the places he'd seen, the things he'd done. He had been away and he had seen the elephant and he was back. They all recognized a toughness about him that he had lacked eight years ago; they recognized it and never tested it, and they liked him because he didn't make a show of it.

If there was a shooting match, or a Sunday afternoon rodeo at one of the ranches, or an impromptu wrestling match, Al participated and took top honors. As the weeks passed, the Hole people began to wonder when he'd mosey on. A little jealousy developed here and there among the men, partly over his demonstrated superiority, partly because several of the girls made no secret of their admiration for him. He sensed it was time to drift along, to nowhere in particular, with nothing to do in particular, and then, suddenly, he reaped a dividend he had not expected.

He was standing beside a corral gate at the Diamond A, waiting to ride a bad horse named Sunbeam, a horse that no one else had been able to ride, when he heard a stranger talking. The man's name was So Long Joe, or at least that was all the name he claimed. He had been in the Hole about a week, saying it had got too hot for him in the San Juans where he'd spent the winter. Although the day of the Wild Bunch was long past, the Hole still served as a refuge for men who were on the run and needed to stop and catch their breath.

So Long Joe was a teller of tall tales, and Al was never sure what was truth and what was a lie. But now he caught the word Purvis and he swung toward the man, attention fixed sharply upon the story So Long Joe was telling.

"This lawyer was a tall drink of water if I ever seen one," So Long Joe was saying, "a cold fish who could look right through you and see the collar button on the back of your neck, but by God, he was smart. I shot this gambler all right. I caught him dealing crooked and I beat him to the draw. They had no right to hold me for murder, but some friends of his done it just the same. It didn't do no good, though. Hell, when Purvis got done cross-examining the witnesses who was trying to get me hung, he had 'em turned inside out.

"The jury let me go, but I didn't have no money to pay Purvis. He says to me you'd better get it by three o'clock tomorrow. I says I'll have it. You be at the south edge of town right above the falls, and I'll give it to you. He says I'll be there.

"Well, I figured the place to get money was from the bank, so I used my .45 for collateral, had 'em count out $500, which was what Purvis said I owed him, and I rode out of town with it. Purvis was standing right where I told him to be. I tossed the dinero to him and said so long and kept on riding. I stayed ahead of the posse, all right, and I sure wasn't going back to find out, but I'll bet that bastard stuck the money in his pocket. It was in a canvas sack marked Fortune State Bank, so he knowed where and how I got it."

Al walked up to the man. "What was this Purvis's first name?"

"Ronald, I think it was. Yeah, I'm sure that was it. Why?"

"Was he married?"

"Yeah, he sure was. His wife used to come to court with him. The best damned looking woman I ever seen. Just one squint at her was enough to make a man want . . ."

"You know her name?"

"I heard him call her by name once." So Long Joe scratched his head and frowned. "Lemme see. Janet? No, that ain't quite right. Janice. That was it. Yeah, I'm sure it was. Why?"

"Where is this town of Fortune?"

"Above Ouray. Purty close to Red Mountain. Why?"

Al turned and walked toward his horse. Someone yelled, "Al, ain't you gonna ride Sunbeam?"

"Later," he said, and mounting, rode away.

CHAPTER IX

As Lincoln Drews climbed the hill to the Purvis house, the thought occurred to him that the banker was a weak man. A strong man with any sense of inner security, of real self-confidence, would not have to build a sprawling brick house above the town; he would not have to plant a fine lawn and enclose it with an iron fence, and entertain lavishly, and set a huge bronze deer in front of the house for everyone to see and admire. But perhaps it wasn't weakness. Only vanity. Or self-adulation.

As Drews stepped across the porch toward the front door, he considered the standards by which Ronald Purvis selected the social elite who had been entertained in his house. There were the Charnleys, and the Whipples, and the Bentleys, and a few others such as Dr. Chute, and Frank McClain who owned the Mercantile, and a few prosperous ranchers.

Not the rich necessarily. Or the social climbers. Or those who occupied a prestige position in the community, although all of these might be part of the standard. Mostly, it seemed to Drews that Purvis picked people who played to his vanity, and who accepted him as the community leader. But Lincoln Drews, a bachelor with little money and no particular social status was excluded, probably because he was too hardheaded, too much of a maverick. He wondered with wry amusement what Purvis would do if he knew his wife was entertaining him at dinner.

As he jerked the bell pull, he thought of the rumor that had spread all over town, when the house was built, that every door knob was gold-plated. He glanced at the knob to the left of the bell pull. Sure enough, it was gold-plated, the plating having worn through in a few places to the base metal beneath.

The door opened and Maggie Nolan, the Purvis housekeeper, said, "Come in, Mr. Drews."

He stepped inside and hung his hat on the hall tree. Maggie motioned toward the crimson portieres that separated the hall from the parlor. "Make yourself at home, Mr. Drews. I'll tell Mrs. Purvis you're here."

"Thank you, Maggie," Drews said, and stepping through the doorway, glanced around the big room.

Again it was with wry amusement that he considered the fact that he was the only professional man in Dead Horse who had not been here, and he was here now only because Mrs. Purvis, for some reason which he still did not understand, had suddenly felt a strong need for his services.

The room was a cold and formal one to Drews's way of thinking. The curtains at the windows were made of Battenburg lace, the drapes of yellow brocaded satin. The oak paneling of the walls ran to the ceiling; the thick Brussels carpet under his feet was blue, so dark it seemed almost black. A number of pictures hung from the wall, most of them too somber for Drews's taste. Only one attracted his interest, a Prang chromo with the title, "Why Doesn't He Come?"

Drews sat down on a divan between two front windows. An expensive house, he thought, as out of place in Dead Horse as the Prang chromo was out of the place on the wall. This room, with its luxurious furnishings, fitted Ronald Purvis's cold personality with perfection; it did not fit Mrs. Purvis's at all. He wondered if she had been permitted to furnish any of the rooms.

Knowing the manner in which Purvis demanded compliance from everyone around him, Drews had a feeling that Janice had not been given the privilege of selecting the furnishings for any of the rooms. His gaze strayed to the chromo on the wall. Perhaps she had chosen it, he thought. It was the kind of colorful thing she would pick, and it certainly was not in keeping with the rest of the room.

He heard her on the stairs a moment later and glanced at his watch. Nearly half past twelve. He had talked to Al Cobb longer than he had intended.

She came into the room from the hall, moving with quick grace. She held her hand out to him, saying, "I'm so glad you could come, Mr. Drews."

He rose and took her hand, sensing the emotional strain under which she labored, even more than he had that morning in his office. He said, "I apologize for being late. I took more time in jail than I expected."

"It's quite all right," she said. "I think dinner is ready. Let me ask Maggie."

She disappeared into the dining room. He watched her walk away from him, thinking that although she had changed to a black skirt and white shirtwaist with a severe, high collar, she could not disguise the rich maturity and perfection of her figure.

She was a woman who needed love and who, in turn, had a great capacity for returning a man's love, with every nerve and fiber of her beautiful body. She did not belong in this house; by her very nature she did not belong to Ronald Purvis, and Drews wondered what crazy chain of circumstances had induced her to marry him. In that moment, Lincoln Drews realized he hated Ronald Purvis, a discovery that startled him because it seemed utterly irrational, striking him as it did at this moment.

Janice returned, saying, "Will you come, Mr. Drews?

Maggie says dinner is ready."

He followed her into the dining room. Jerry stood straight-backed and sober at the end of the table, gravely considering Drews as he approached. His round, handsome face had a freshly scrubbed look about it; his curly blond hair had been dampened and roached above his forehead.

"Mr. Drews, I want you to meet my son, Jerry," Janice said. "Jerry, this is our guest, Mr. Lincoln Drews."

Drews held out his hand and gripped Jerry's small one. "How are you, Jerry?"

"Fine," Jerry answered. "How are you?"

"I'm fine, too," Drews said, "except for being hungry."

"We'll fix that," Janice said.

She lifted the boy to his tall-legged chair and sat down beside him, Drews holding her chair for her. "Thank you," she murmured, and motioned for him to sit across from her.

The Ironstone plates depicted a hunting scene of a man riding a horse, a hound beside him, with other men on horses in the distance jumping a fence.

Jerry pointed at his plate. "I get a horse," he said. "Mamma said I would."

"Then you surely will," Drews said.

"I went hunting," Jerry announced.

"For bears?" Drews asked.

"No. Mice."

Janice smiled as she cut a small piece of steak on Jerry's plate into bites. "Lena Walker looks after him in the daytime," she said. "You know, Pete Walker's daughter."

Drews nodded. Pete was an old, crippled-up cowhand who owned the livery stable. He was in debt, having bought it with a small down payment and having contracted to make heavy monthly installments. So he was glad for Lena to have a job, but he had told Drews more than once that he wished she could find work somewhere else. "Mrs. Purvis is all right," old Pete had said, "and the boy's a good little kid, but that damned Purvis treats Lena like a servant. By God, she wasn't hired to wait on him." But jobs were scarce in Dead Horse, so she continued taking care of Jerry.

"Lena is awfully good with Jerry," Janice said. "They go up into the mow of the barn and move the hay. That makes the mice run and Jerry chases them with a stick." Janice grimaced. "I don't know how Lena can do it. Mice scare me. One time a mouse ran up her leg. I'd die if that ever happened to me."

Jerry giggled in delight. "She hollered and jumped up and down."

"I'll bet she did," Drews said.

After that the conversation lapsed into small talk about the weather and how good the custard was. When Jerry finished, he said, "I want down."

Janice wiped his face with his napkin and pulled his chair back. He put his arms up and hugged her, then slid off the chair and ran into the kitchen to find Lena. For a moment Janice kept her back to Drews, and when she turned, he saw that she was close to crying. She shook her head, trying to smile and not quite succeeding.

"I don't know what's the matter with me any more," she said. "I took him too much for granted until he was stolen, and then since Al brought him back, everything he does breaks me up. Sometimes he says, 'I love you,' only he has trouble with his l's and it usually comes out, 'I wuv you.'"

She rose and going to the cherry-wood sideboard, picked up a box of cigars and offered them to Drews. "I know you smoke a pipe, but perhaps you'd like a cigar. I understand these are very expensive Havanas." She paused, and added with a trace of bitterness in her voice, "Ronald says they are the only luxuries he permits himself."

Drews took one, asking, "You don't mind if I smoke?"

"Not at all." She motioned toward the parlor. "Let's go where we'll be more comfortable."

She shut the door behind them and motioned for Drews to sit down. Drews lighted his cigar and, walking across the room, sat on the divan between the two windows. He said, "Jerry's a fine little boy. You have every right to be proud of him."

"I am," she said. "When I think about what might have happened to him, or what still might happen, I almost lose my mind. That's why I went to you for help this morning, as much as wanting to get Al off. What did he tell you?"

"Very little that I didn't already know," Drews answered. "Something occurred to me just now. I didn't think it was wise to ask Jerry, but has he been able to tell you anything about who kidnapped him? I guess we all assumed he was too much of a baby to testify in court, but he talks pretty well."

She shook her head. "He hasn't been able to tell me

anything more than we knew. He wandered off that afternoon behind the barn. Somewhere down the alley a man on a horse picked him up and carried him off. He didn't go far. As near as I can tell, they went into a shed and stayed until dark. I suppose the man was afraid they'd be seen. Jerry doesn't know who he was. You see, he didn't know Lee Fawcett. I had thought of taking him to see Fawcett's body, but it would have been too much of a shock."

Drews nodded. "Judge Charnley wouldn't have admitted his testimony, anyway."

Janice sat with her hands folded on her lap. She said, "It has been a terrible experience for Jerry. He didn't sleep for more than a few minutes at a time for a week or more, after Al brought him back. He'd wake up and scream and talk about the mean man, and I couldn't do anything but hold him in my arms, and tell him he was safe, and the mean man wouldn't get him again. Even to save Al's life, I couldn't keep asking Jerry questions. I wanted him to forget it if he could. Just the last few days he acts natural, as if he is forgetting it. Now tell me what Al said."

"He hit on one interesting notion that I'd thought about," Drews said, "but I could never make any sense out of it, and neither has Al. He said he was riding through the country coming up from Rawlins, and met a search party that Fred Bentley was running. He says why did Bentley overlook the cabin where Jerry was, as close to town as it is?"

She was silent as she turned the question over in her mind, then said, "Did you ask Bentley?"

Drews nodded. "I asked him when I first took the case, but I don't know that his answer was an honest one. He said no kidnapper would be fool enough to hide the boy so close to town, so he didn't bother to look there."

"Are you trying to say that Bentley and Fawcett were in this together?" she asked.

"It's an idea, but there's no way we can prove it," he said. "Bentley certainly won't admit it." He hesitated, then added, "I knew Fawcett pretty well. He wasn't real smart, not smart enough to think up something himself. He always looked to Bentley or someone else for orders."

She stared at her hands, a pulse beginning to throb in her forehead. "What else did Al say?"

Drews took the cigar out of his mouth and rolled it between thumb and forefinger. An expensive cigar, he told himself, one that would have cost a dollar if he had bought it in the Stockman's Bar. He said, "Nothing that was really pertinent. I asked him to go over it again, but he told me the same story he's told a dozen times. I kept after him, and finally he said he'd been sent to the reform school when he was sixteen, that you and he and your husband had grown up together in a small town in Nebraska, and both of them liked you. When he got out, he went back to see you and you acted as if you were glad to see him. You kissed him, then Ronald came out of the house and tried to hit him, but he hit Purvis and knocked him over a porch railing. You thought he was dead and told Al to run. He did, because he knew what they'd do to him if they caught him."

"That's all?"

Drews nodded. "Doesn't help much, does it? I think there's more and you're the one who'll have to tell it."

She rose, more agitated than at any other time he had seen her. She said, "Go back to your office, Mr. Drews. I'm going to get a hotel room. Bentley will hear about it and come to me. I'll find out what he knows. I want you to be listening outside in the hall so I'll have a witness. I don't know how you'll know when he's coming, but I suppose he'll wait until after dark."

He was being dismissed, but he wasn't ready to go. He rose and walked to her. He said, "Mrs. Purvis . . ."

"Would you mind calling me Janice?"

"I'd like to. Janice, I think there is something important Al left out and you can tell me what it is."

"Nothing that you'd call pertinent."

"Then I'll go to Purvis and ask him," Drews said. "I've never asked him why he hates Al, but he does or he wouldn't have given that statement to Whipple. Maybe knocking him over the porch railing that time was enough. Maybe he's still jealous of Al. But I want to know."

"That's it," she said eagerly. "That's the whole thing. Our marriage has been a failure. Ronnie and I hate each other. We have for a long time. I've wished so many times I had married Al."

He took her hands and looked at her, but she turned her face from him as if afraid he would read something there she did not want him to know. He said, "Janice, Al's a hard man. I've talked to him a great deal about his past. He's told me everything, I guess, except what I really need to know. He's been to a lot of places. He's done a lot of things. Do you think you could have lived his kind of life and been happy?"

She drew her hands from his and walked toward the hall. "You'll hear from me later this afternoon. Whatever you do, don't go to my husband and start asking a lot of questions. You'll just make things worse."

There was nothing for him to do then but leave. He was halfway down the hill when he remembered something she'd said, that didn't seem logical—that she had come to him for help that morning because of what might still happen to Jerry as much as to get Al off.

The more he thought about it, the less sense it made.

Fawcett was dead. If Fred Bentley had thought the kidnapping up as a means of extorting money from Ronald Purvis, and Fawcett had simply been a tool who carried out Bentley's scheme, he wouldn't be stupid enough to try again. Bentley was a lot of things, but Drews would never call him stupid.

By the time he reached his office, he still had not made any sense out of it.

CHAPTER X

USUALLY Alexander Whipple was very talkative when he ate dinner with his wife, but today he was withdrawn and silent. His wife covertly watched him, worrying, and although she often felt she wanted to scream at him to shut up, today for some perverse reason she wished she could think of something to prime the pump. Like many childless couples, they had no one but each other, and because his behavior today was anything but normal, she decided he must be sick.

Finally, as Whipple finished his third cup of coffee and picked up his half-chewed cigar which he had laid on the table beside his plate, Mrs. Whipple could stand it no longer. She said, "Alex, you haven't said three words since you got home. Are you sick or mad at me or what?"

"No." He chewed on his cigar, half angry at her question, and half pleased, too, because he would have felt neglected if she didn't fuss over him. He started to get up, then dropped back into his chair. "I guess I'm a little sick at that. I've been hearing talk that Ronald Purvis is going to run against me for the legislature."

"He wouldn't do that, Alex," she said horrified. "Not without talking to you about it."

"He might," Whipple said. "Fact is, he would if he thought he could make money out of being in the legislature. He's a cold, calculating son of a bitch."

"Alex," she said reprovingly.

"Well, that's what he is," Whipple insisted. "With the money he's got he might beat me, too. He might even get the Governor on his side."

"No, Alex. You're just imagining things and you're getting yourself all upset. You've always supported the governor's program. Besides, he's your friend."

"Until a better one comes along," Whipple said sourly. "No use fooling ourselves, Madge. A man like Purvis, who's got brains and money, can get just about anything he wants."

"But nobody likes him."

"Nobody has to. When a man's got brains, he can

figure out what he can buy, and then if he's got the money, he can go ahead and buy it." He scowled at his wife. "I've always been a good party man, and the *Bugle* has been the leading party newspaper for years in this section of Wyoming, but that doesn't count if somebody else comes along who's more important. Purvis is young and ambitious and rich. You can't beat that combination."

His wife was silent for a moment, wanting to reassure him, but knowing that he was right in everything he had said. Finally she asked, "Why don't you come right out and pin him down? You have a right to know."

"I sure do. Well, I've been thinking about asking him, but I'm kind of scared. He can be as nasty as hell when he sets his mind to it." He rose, then stood looking down at his wife. "Madge, I was talking to Linc Drews this morning. He suggested that I run for Congress."

"Why, that would be fine." She hesitated, not wanting to hurt him but thinking it was a totally impractical notion. "But it takes so much money to run for an office like that. You'd have to travel all over the state."

"And *you'd* have to get the paper out." He picked up his derby and put it on, gave his cigar a couple of chews, and added, "I just might scare the hell out of a few people, though."

He stooped to kiss her, taking the cigar out of his mouth barely in time, and walked out, leaving a wet fragment of tobacco on her lower lip. He walked toward Main Street slowly, thinking that when a man bucked Ronald Purvis, he was taking on a giant, and Alexander knew all too well that he was not a giant killer. But that seat in the state legislature was sacred to him; it was the one tiny dot he had made on the huge scroll of history, and he didn't want it erased.

Lincoln Drews was a popular man in the county and a respected man in state politics, but how much help he would be in an open fight with Purvis was a question in Whipple's mind. He considered himself a realist, and the more he thought about it, the surer he was that Purvis would plow Drews under in one way or another. Still, if Purvis was after his seat, Whipple would rather have Drews for an ally than anyone else in Dead Horse County.

Whipple had newspaper-men friends in different parts of the state, and Drews had lawyer friends in different parts of the state. If Drews pulled a rabbit out of his hat and freed Al Cobb at the last minute, he'd be one of the best-known lawyers in Wyoming. The more he thought about it, the more certain he was, as he had told his wife, that he could scare the hell out of some people if he decided to try for Congress.

He stepped into the bank, nodded at Augie Nolan, the teller, and asked, "Mr. Purvis in?"

"He's back in his office." Nolan motioned toward the door marked "Private" in the rear. "He's alone. Go ahead if you want to see him."

Whipple pushed open the gate beside the teller's cage, stepped through it, and walked on back to Purvis's office. He knocked and opened the door when Purvis called, "Come in."

The banker sat at his desk thumbing through a pile of documents. He glanced up, saw who it was, and rose.

"I'm glad to see you, Alex," he said, and held out his hand. "Come on in and sit down."

Whipple shut the door, shook Purvis's hand, and sat down. The banker was as tall as Drews, but he gave the impression of being much taller because he was extremely thin. He eased back into his swivel chair and, opening a box of cigars, held it out to Whipple.

"Have a good cigar, Alex," he said. "These are Havanas, the best I can buy. My one luxury."

"Thank you," Whipple said.

He took a cigar, amused that Purvis would say he had just one luxury. He had the best house in town, the most expensive furniture, the finest yard, and the most beautiful wife. Wife! Whipple had completely forgotten what Drews had told him that morning.

Ronald Purvis always gave the impression of being the master of every problem that faced him, of being indestructible and unbeatable and immovable, but now Whipple knew with grim certainty that he had the means of beating Purvis if he had to, that his wife was the one chink in his armor.

"I was going to see you if you hadn't dropped in," Purvis said. "I presume you have something in this week's *Bugle* about our irrigation project."

"I do indeed." Whipple felt a sudden surge of strength that he had never experienced before when he had faced this man. "I finished it just before dinner. I played up the future picture of Dead Horse County when the flood of farmers comes in. New construction. New businesses. More trade for the established firms. Higher real estate values. Possibly a stub line from the Union Pacific."

"Certainly, not possibly," Purvis reproved.

"All right, I'll change the word." Whipple chewed on the cigar, thinking that it didn't taste any better than the nickel cigars he bought in the Stockman's Bar. Again he thought of what Drews had said about Purvis's wife. It was a time bomb—not a weapon he could use at the moment—because of his promise to Drews. Still, it was comforting to know that this confident man who sat across the desk from him had a weak spot. He said, "One thing occurs to me, Ronald. We'll put 20,000 acres under the ditch, but it's all winter range for half a dozen cow outfits. They'll raise hell when they see this project is going to materialize."

"Not for long, Alex." Purvis removed his pince-nez glasses and rubbed his nose. "I was going over the mortgages that the bank owns. Last year was a dry year as you know. Prices were down, too. This year doesn't look any better. Everybody in town is hurting. You have no idea how much the stores are carrying on their books. I can't think of more than three outfits that aren't mortgaged to the bank for every cent they're worth and more. They aren't in a position to bother us."

"I didn't realize that," Whipple said.

Purvis replaced his glasses and smiled his superior smile. "Your job is to keep tooting the horn just as you have been. This project will cost about $100,000. I plan to put up half. It's up to men like you and Fred Bentley, and Linc Drews, and Doc Chute to raise the balance."

This seemed to Whipple to be strictly a dream. No one in the county besides Purvis had that kind of money, but there seemed to be no point in raising the question. He said, "There's one thing more, Ronald. I've heard talk that you were planning to run against me for the legislature."

Purvis smiled again. For years Whipple had made a habit of observing the way men smiled. In Purvis's case, it was a strange curling of his thin lips that touched no other part of his ascetic face. When Whipple tried to think of adjectives that described the banker, he could think of nothing except words such as cold, or chill, or ice. That was exactly what his eyes were when he smiled, pale-green ice.

"Why yes, I was planning to run for the legislature," Purvis said. "I have been aiming to talk to you about it. It won't hurt your career to sit out one term, and I promise that you'll be back in the legislature after I've served the one term, and only one. You see, I'm going for the State Senate later. Let's say this is just a stepping stone for me. I will, of course, expect the support of the *Bugle*."

"Suppose I run against you?"

Purvis shrugged his thin shoulders, and, setting his elbows on the desk, laced his fingers together. "Let's just say I don't advise it."

Whipple leaned forward. "We could make a deal. I'll support you for the legislature if you support me for Congress."

"Congress!" The word was jolted out of Purvis. For a moment he was startled, then he laughed aloud. "No deal, Alex, and I advise you against trying for Congress."

Whipple rose, so furious he stopped thinking coherently for the moment. "You can't do this, Ronald. By God, if you want a fight, you'll get it."

"All right," Purvis said indifferently. "Just remember one thing. I can bring in a good newspaper man and set him up and you'll be out of business in six months."

"You can't do that, either. I've had the *Bugle* for 20 years." Whipple stopped, his mind working again. This was exactly what Purvis would and could do if he wasn't destroyed, and in that instant Whipple knew he was fighting for his political and business life. He said slowly, "You going to the hanging tomorrow?"

Purvis rose and stood as rigid as if he had been frozen there behind his desk. He said, "No." One word. No more, but it told Whipple that this was the end of the partnership that dated back to the day Purvis had bought the bank and moved to Dead Horse. Now Whipple had to be a giant killer.

"One thing Linc Drews and I were wondering about," Whipple said. "You gave me a statement about Al Cobb the day he was found guilty. What you said, and the way you said it, made it clear you hated him. Not just ordinary hate, but something pretty damned personal. Why?"

Now Whipple saw something he had not believed possible. Purvis's face was normally pale, but it turned red, quickly and violently, so red that it looked as if he had been out in the sun too long, and the skin had been burned to the place where it would break out into blisters. For a moment Purvis didn't move, then he jerked a desk drawer open and picked up a pistol. He thumbed the hammer back as he whispered, "Get out. If you're not out of here in ten seconds, I'll kill you."

Whipple's life had been threatened more than once, but he realized instantly he had never been as close to death as he was now. For several seconds he couldn't move; he was completely paralyzed by fear. He stood there staring at Purvis, then he came alive, his teeth snapping together so sharply that he bit the cigar in two, the part outside his mouth dropping to the floor, the other part going down his throat in a single, convulsive swallow.

He wheeled, he yanked the door open and rushed out of the office. He ran full length into a fat woman who had just entered the bank. He bounced off her, and for what seemed an endless period of time he couldn't get his feet untracked. He didn't take time to look behind, but he had a terrifying feeling that Purvis was coming after him, the cocked gun in his hand.

He dived forward past the fat woman, who was heaving and choking in her anger at being bumped into in this manner, then he was outside and running down the street. He didn't stop until he reached the building that housed Lincoln Drews's office, then he looked back. Purvis was not in sight.

Whipple took a long breath, climbed the stairs and sat down in Drews's office to wait for the lawyer to return. Several minutes passed before he realized that in his terror he had wet his pants, the first time since he had been a small child.

CHAPTER XI

WHEN Drews reached his office, he found Alexander Whipple waiting for him. He stared at the editor in amazement. Whipple was a banty of a man with a great deal of natural bounce, often over-eager and too anxious to please. Now he sat hunched forward in his chair, his legs squeezed together, his derby on the floor beside him.

Whipple's hair was disheveled, as if he had been running his hand through it time after time. Usually the skin of his face was the healthy pink of a child, but now it was the pallid gray of an old man who imagines that death is waiting for him just around the corner.

"What the hell, Alex?" Drews said. "You're the perfect picture of a man who was sent for and couldn't come."

"I just about couldn't." Whipple wet his lips with the tip of his tongue. "Shut the door." When Drews obeyed, Whipple said, "I know something you don't. Ronald Purvis is as crazy as a hydrophobic skunk. He tried to kill me."

Drews walked across the room to his desk and sat down. He said, "Tell me about it, Alex."

Whipple told him what had happened, then added, "I know I'm not any hero, Linc. I haven't always been honest enough to stand for things I believed in. Sometimes I've sucked around after men like Purvis that I thought would do me some good."

He scrubbed his face with both hands, as if trying to remove some memories he would like to forget, then he went on, "But I haven't been so bad, either, compared to most men I know. I have stood for some things in my time, and I always worked like hell for Dead Horse County when I was in the legislature."

"Nobody's accused you of anything," Drews said, wondering why Whipple had suddenly become so defensive.

"I know, I know," Whipple said shrilly. "It's just that I know I've got to fight now, and the chances are it'll be nobody but you and me. I say Purvis is crazy, and that makes him all the more dangerous. I've had my life threatened more than once, Linc, but I was never as scared as I was a while ago, because I'd never had a man point a gun at me before who really intended to kill me. Purvis did, Linc. I swear to God he did."

"I believe you, Alex." Drews took his pipe and tobacco from a coat pocket and filled the pipe. "Purvis isn't crazy. He's probably got the sharpest mind of any man I ever ran into, but certain things like your question about hating Cobb get him out of whack. For a little while he's not rational. We're all that way about some things. For instance, you aren't logical about losing your seat in the legislature."

"No, I guess not," Whipple said glumly. "I know damned well I'm not logical about going to Congress, either. I've just been fooling myself. That's why Purvis laughed at me. Hell, even my wife knew it when I was home at noon and we talked about it."

"It's a bridge we can cross when we get to it," Drews said. "Right now, Al Cobb is our problem. We still don't know the whole story. Cobb doesn't want to die, but he won't tell it. Janice Purvis knows it and she wants to save him, but she won't tell it. You asked Purvis why he hates Cobb and he goes wild. Somewhere we've got to get the link that's missing." He glanced at the clock on the wall. "We've got a little less than 22 hours to get it."

"Not much time," Whipple said. "You know, Linc, when you propositioned me this morning in the Stockman's Bar, I didn't figure to go whole hog with you."

Drews smiled briefly. "That's what I thought. It's always easier to follow a familiar path than it is to strike out across new country. Taking Purvis's orders has become a habit with you, the way it has with almost everybody else in town."

"Well, I'm with you now," Whipple said. "I don't have any choice."

"Let's take another look at this, Alex." Drews leaned back and pulled on his pipe. "When I walked up the hill to Purvis's house at noon, I said to myself he was a weak man or he wouldn't have to make a show of his money the way he does. I was wrong. He's not weak any more than he's crazy. I think he's just awful damned vain and self-centered. Actually he's very strong in his own way. If he goes crazy at times the way he did with you, he's all the more dangerous, as you just said. It's something we have to watch out for."

Drews pulled on his pipe, his eyes half closed. "I judge he's always had things go his way. He's probably been too smart for his own good, and he's had too much money for his own good; therefore he's never had to compromise or consider other people's rights the way the rest of us have. That's what makes him dangerous. In his opinion, the only way of looking at things is his way.

"Right now, he's in the driver's seat. If he sits tight, Al Cobb will hang, and there's nothing you and I can do about it. Nobody else is really interested one way or the other. Judge Charnley is out of town and we can't reach him. He wouldn't do anything if he was here. Most people are like Doc Chute, and Frank McClain, and old Pete Walker. Maybe they don't like Purvis, but they won't buck him, either. It's too dangerous. Besides, why should they do anything for a man like Al Cobb?"

Whipple nodded. "You haven't said anything I can argue with, but you haven't said anything new, either."

Drews laughed shortly. "You're entirely right, Alex. I'm just thinking out loud. The truth is I feel pretty frustrated, with time running out the way it is. Mrs. Purvis is still bound to work on Bentley. He knows something we don't, but I'm not sure that she or either one of us can get it out of him. Fred's best interest is to stick with Purvis, and that's what he'll do."

"One funny angle is Lee Fawcett," Whipple said. "He was a bully and nobody much liked him, but nobody hated him, either, unless they'd had trouble with the law. The men in town who could help Cobb hadn't."

Drews took his pipe out of his mouth. He said thoughtfully, "I quote, 'Our own beloved Deputy Sheriff Lee Fawcett.' He was never beloved alive, but he became beloved in the columns of the august *Weekly Bugle* after he was shot to death by Al Cobb."

Whipple's face turned red. "You won't let me forget that, will you? I don't know why I mentioned him."

"You wrote that before you changed sides," Drews reminded him. "You expressed the sentiment of almost everybody in Dead Horse because Lee Fawcett, yesterday's bully, had become today's martyr. Al Cobb, a stranger with the reputation of a bad man, was the killer and he must hang. Public sentiment hasn't changed, Alex. We're alone, you and I and Janice Purvis."

Whipple shifted his weight in his chair. "I don't see that there's anything we can do."

"We wait," Drews said. "Time's running out, but we wait."

"For what?"

"For Mrs. Purvis to get something out of Fred Bentley. A small chance, but a chance." Drews laid his pipe on his desk and leaned back, his hands laced behind his head. "There's one more chance and I think it's a better one. That's Purvis himself. He's determined that Cobb is going to hang. We don't know why, but we may find out before noon tomorrow. I still say it has something to do with him and his wife and Cobb, something more important than the trouble they had in Nebraska when they were kids. Or young people anyway. Purvis is afraid, or he wouldn't perform the way he did with you, so we know Cobb is his sore spot. If you or I or his wife can squeeze hard enough on that sore spot, he'll do something else that's as crazy as threatening to kill you. When he does, we've got him."

"You're wishing for the moon," Whipple grumbled.

"I can't think of anything else to wish for," Drews said, "but don't forget one thing. We destroy Purvis or let him destroy himself, if we're going to save Cobb. When we

90

do, you won't have any trouble going back to the legislature."

"Or saving my newspaper," Whipple said bitterly. "He
even threatened to bring in another man and set up a
rival paper. He told me he'd have me out of business in
six months."

"And he might do it," Drews said.

"He sure as hell might," Whipple agreed. "Well, I'm
going home. When I come back, I'll have a revolver in
my pocket."

"I've got to sit here till I hear from Mrs. Purvis,"
Drews said. "I want to see you before you go home for
the evening."

Whipple nodded and left the office. Drews rose and,
moving to a window, stared down into the dusty street.
He was not a man who by nature was geared for waiting.
Now, with every nerve in his body being pulled tighter
each passing minute, he wasn't sure he could keep on
waiting.

CHAPTER XII

JANICE PURVIS stood by the window watching Lin-
coln Drews until he disappeared down the hill.
Before she had gone to his office this morning, her
acquaintance with him had been merely a speaking one.
She remembered meeting him at a supper at Judge
Charnley's house, not long after she had first moved to
Dead Horse, and she had been well impressed by him
then.

More than once she had suggested to Ronnie that they

include Drews when they were giving a Sunday dinner or having a party, but he had always said no, the last time so curtly that for the sake of peace she had stopped mentioning Drews. Ronnie had never given any explanation. She had often wondered about it, because Drews was the only man of any prominence in Dead Horse who had never been invited to the Purvis home.

Now, looking at Drews's broad back as he strode down the hill, she felt that in these few hours she had learned to know him well. She liked the way he held his head, the square cut of his shoulders. In a way he reminded her of Al Cobb, although his face was rough hewn, not at all handsome in the way Al's was. The resemblance was something much more intangible, having to do with the spirit of the two men rather than their physical appearance.

She considered it a moment before she could put her finger on the similarity. Finally she decided they were both by nature rebels. Each had his set of standards that were very much different, but the two men were alike in the sense that neither would conform simply because it was the easy way. The thought brought some comfort to her, for with it came the certainty that Drews would go on fighting for Al Cobb right down to the moment of the hanging, in spite of all the pressure Ronnie could bring to bear upon him.

Now Janice thought she understood why Ronnie had refused to invite Drews to his home. Ronnie had an uncanny talent for sizing up men, just as he had a talent for making money. He wanted nothing to do with a maverick, and Drews, she was sure, was a man who would make his own decisions regardless of how much profit there would be in going along with Ronnie. Not that Ronnie had ever said it in words, but she did not doubt that he had measured Drews during the first weeks he had been in Dead Horse, and had found him wanting.

She turned from the window and went upstairs to her room. She had decided upon her course of action that morning and nothing had happened to change her mind. What she was planning to do would not be pleasant or easy. She had made her decision simply because she could not think of any other place to start.

Quickly she packed her suitcase with enough clothes to last a week. She took off the skirt and shirtwaist she was wearing, deciding that the costume was too severe for her purpose, and put on a dark skirt and a blouse of lighter blue, an outfit that made the most of her figure but was not too revealing.

She hesitated a moment, then reluctantly took a silk nightgown and lace negligee from a bureau drawer and, dropping them into her suitcase, closed the lid. She had long ago learned she appealed to men, so much so that there were some she did not dare encourage with as much as a single word, or gesture, or smile. Fred Bentley, she was sure, was such a man. He was coarse, vulgar, and conceited, holding absolutely no appeal for her, but she must act as if he did.

She opened her closet door and, moving a pile of hat-boxes in the far corner, felt around in the darkness until she found a buckskin purse filled with money, both gold and greenbacks. She shoved the hatboxes into place and backed out of the closet, then dropped the purse into her reticule. She did not take time to count the money. She knew she had a little over $500, money she had saved laboriously over the years for just such an emergency as she faced now.

Ronnie had never given her an allowance or any money for her own use, unless she told him exactly what she wanted it for. It was from these sums that she had saved this pittance, buying closely and telling Ronnie she had spent all he had given her.

Her father had died just before they moved to Dead Horse, leaving her nothing. Or so Ronnie said. He took care of the Hart estate, and after the funeral in Royal, he told her he'd had to pay for the coffin himself, that the store and the house were mortgaged for more than they were worth. She'd thought he was lying and still did, but she had no head for business and didn't know how to go at finding the truth.

For a moment she stood looking around the room, thinking that what she was doing today would make retreat impossible. She would never come back to this house to live. She would move to Rawlins, or Laramie, or maybe Cheyenne. She would have to find something to do to support herself and Jerry.

Perhaps Al would ask her to go with him if he was freed, but she dismissed the possibility at once. There had been a time when she would gladly have gone with Al, but not now. Drews had asked her if she could accept Al's way of life. She had avoided answering him, but she knew the answer. She couldn't. She didn't try to analyze her reasons. She simply knew that Jerry must be raised in a different environment than Al Cobb could give him.

Turning to the bureau, she picked up the gold watch that Ronnie had given her for Christmas many years before, and pinned it on her blouse over her left breast. She put on a hat, one she had selected before dinner; it was easier to manage than her wide-brimmed hats with their plumes and ornaments. This one was called the Mascotte, a small, Frenchified turban that had been in style a few years ago, and had been a favorite walking hat for street wear.

The fact that the hat was out of style made little difference in Dead Horse. If anything, it was an advantage. That was one of the things Ronnie had warned her about when they had moved here. She must not look too chic, or she would make Mrs. Charnley, and Mrs. Bentley, and Mrs. Whipple, and the others look dowdy. Ronnie knew as well as she did that anything she wore would make them look dowdy by comparison, for that was the kind of women they were, but at least it was something about which she had been careful.

She picked up a small bag and slipped into Jerry's room. Usually he did not wake up from his nap until three or later, so she worked silently, not wanting to rouse him. She packed the bag with enough clothes to last him for three days, then she stood at the head of his bed looking down at him, so filled with emotion that for a time it was hard to hold back the tears. She wanted to kneel beside the bed and hold him in her arms, to kiss him and feel his moist lips on her cheek; but she must not wake him.

She thought: *If it hadn't been for Al, Jerry might be dead. For saving Jerry they are going to hang him.*

The tears came then in spite of anything she could do. Quickly she left the room, closing the door behind her. She set the bag down and waited until she stopped crying. She wiped her eyes, and prayed that she would be given the wisdom and the strength that was necessary to save Al's life, to cheat and lie if that was what it took, even to giving herself to Fred Bentley.

She went down the stairs to the kitchen and called, "Lena."

The girl was helping Maggie Nolan, but she came quickly when she heard Janice. When she appeared in the doorway, Janice said, "Will you come upstairs, please? There's something I want you to do."

"Yes, ma'am," Lena said.

Janice turned and climbed the stairs to her room. She waited there until Lena came in. The girl smiled as she said, "You're very pretty this afternoon, Mrs. Purvis."

"Thank you, Lena."

"But you've been crying. Is something wrong?"

"I hoped it didn't show," Janice said. "I'm going away for a little while, Lena, and I need your help. I packed a bag with some of Jerry's things, enough to last three days. I'm sure I won't be gone that long, but if I'm gone any longer, you can wash some out. He's sound asleep. I wanted to pick him up and hug him, but I didn't. I guess I cried a little, just thinking about what had happened to him."

"Yes, ma'am," Lena said. "Sometimes I do, too. He's so precious."

"As soon as he wakes up, I want you to take him home with you. Don't tell anyone where you're going. Not even Maggie. If she asks you, just say you're going for a walk. If anyone comes after him except me, don't give him up. Not to anyone. Do you understand that?"

"Yes, ma'am."

"This may be dangerous. I want you to understand that, too. Do you have any place to hide him, if you need to?"

"Yes, ma'am. We have a cellar under our kitchen. There's a trap door in the floor. I can put a rug over it and nobody will know it's there. I'll tell him it's a game and to be real quiet. I think he will be all right."

Janice wasn't sure he would, but she couldn't think of anything else to do with him, and she was sure Lena would do the best she could.

"You're willing to do this?" Janice asked.

"Yes, ma'am, if you want me to."

"I wouldn't ask you unless it was necessary, but I know you love Jerry almost as much as I do."

"Yes, ma'am, I sure do. I won't let nothing happen to him."

Janice picked up her suitcase and reticule. She said, "Remember. Don't let anyone have Jerry but me. I'll be at the hotel tonight, but don't come after me for anything unless it's an emergency. I'm sure you won't have one, because you take care of him as well as I do. Just tell him I had to go away for a little while."

She left the room and went down the stairs, hoping that Maggie wouldn't see her. The housekeeper was the wife of Augie Nolan, the teller in the bank. Neither, Janice thought, had any great love for Ronnie, but they owed their jobs to him, a fact that would determine their loyalty.

When she reached the base of the hill, she turned into the alley and walked past the rear of the bank, so she would not be in front of it and run the risk of meeting Ronnie, who might be leaving or arriving. Coming to a vacant lot, she followed a path through the weeds to the street and turned into the hotel. Ronnie was not in sight. So far she was lucky.

She rang the bell on the desk. A moment later Harvey Pearson came into the lobby from the dining room. He was a very fat man who walked with a sort of rolling gait. He said to all and sundry, "I take my meals in my dining room. Look at me and see how good the food is. I'm the best advertisement a restaurant can have."

Now he paused, surprised at seeing Janice here. He said, "Howdy, Miz Purvis. You sure are all purtied up today. Can I do something for you?"

"Yes, Harvey, I want a room."

He eyed her suitcase dubiously. "Well now, Miz Purvis, I don't know. I don't have any rooms . . ."

"Forgive my rudeness, Harvey," Janice said, "but I don't believe you. To my knowledge, this hotel has never been filled up in the entire history of Dead Horse."

He grinned amiably. "Well, doggone it, Miz Purvis, I didn't aim to lie to you. I was just trying to say that I didn't have a room fit for you. Nothing like that fine house you have."

"I have money to pay for a room," she said sharply. "I didn't ask for gold-plated door knobs and Brussels carpets. Will you tell me which room I can have and give me a key."

He scratched a droopy cheek, eyeing her thoughtfully. He was asking himself, she decided, why she was here, and how much trouble he would get into with Ronnie if he let her have a room. Finally he said, "All right, Miz Purvis." He went behind the desk and picked a key off the rack. "Room 12 is vacant. It's as good as any I've got."

She snatched the key from his hand and turned toward the stairs. He asked, "What are you doing here, Miz Purvis?"

She whirled to face him. "What I do is my business, Harvey. Not yours or my husband's or anyone else's. Do you understand that?"

"Yes, ma'am." His face turned red and he retreated a step. "Doggone it, Miz Purvis. I didn't aim to make you huffy or nothing, but it does seem kind of peculiar . . ."

She gave him her back and went up the stairs. She would be the most talked-about woman in Dead Horse by evening, she thought, but that was part of the price she had known all the time she would have to pay.

She smiled as she thought about it. Most of the women, particularly the gossipy ones like Mrs. Bentley and Mrs. Chute, would say this was what they had expected all the time, anyhow. They'd known from the first that she wasn't any better than she ought to be. Poor Mrs. Bentley! Perhaps Fred had more reason than any other man in Dead Horse to look around.

She found Room 12 to be in the back overlooking the weed-covered alley. She set her suitcase down inside the door, closed it, and went back downstairs, walking past Harvey Pearson with her head high. She went directly to the bank and said to Augie Nolan, "Please tell my husband I'm here."

Nolan was in the teller's cage waiting on Mrs. Chute. That was perfect, Janice thought. Within a few minutes, the story, fanned by Mrs. Chute's wagging tongue, would spread from one end of Dead Horse to the other. Fred Bentley was bound to hear.

"He's in his office, Mrs. Purvis," Nolan said. "Why don't you just go on back and . . ."

"I'm not going back," she said firmly. "For once he can come to me."

Nolan hesitated, chewing on his lower lip, but Janice was staring hard at him, and he did not have the temerity to stand against her. He walked back to Ronnie's office, knocked on the door, and said something to Ronnie when the door opened. This was the kind of thing she would never do under ordinary circumstances, and it would make him furious. She counted on his fury bringing him to her.

She was right. He strode past Nolan toward the gate at the end of the teller's cage, his icy green eyes sparking with anger. He said, "Janice, what kind of a fool prank is this? All you have to do to see me is to come back . . ."

"This is no prank, Ronnie."

She paused, knowing how much he hated to be called Ronnie in front of people. It sounded juvenile, he said. He had told her repeatedly to call him Ronald. Now she saw the fury take root and grow; she saw scarlet sweep across his face, a sure sign of the insane rage that occasionally took possession of him.

"I'm leaving you, Ronnie," she said, speaking rapidly so he would have no chance to interrupt her. "I've taken a room in the hotel. I want to tell you so there will be no misunderstanding. As long as I've gone this far, I'll tell you one more thing. Lincoln Drews is working on new evidence that will free Al. He'll succeed in spite of anything you can do."

She whirled and walked out, her heels making a sharp, staccato sound on the floor. She went into the hotel, sweeping past Harvey Pearson without a word. When she reached her room, she removed her hat and laid it on the top of the pine bureau. She unpinned the watch from her blouse and snapped it open. The time was one minute after three.

She put a hand to her forehead, feeling the pulse hammer in her temples. If she could only talk to Al, if she could thank him once more for bringing Jerry back . . . but she knew she could not. Perhaps she would never see him again. If she didn't, she hoped that at least he heard she had done all she could for him.

There was so much good in him, so much inherent honesty. He was a hard man, as Lincoln Drews had said, but neither that or anything else justified the fate they had decreed for him. With 21 hours to live, she wondered what thoughts were passing through his mind.

She turned to the bed and stretched out, dreading the time when Fred Bentley would come.

CHAPTER XIII

FOR Lincoln Drews, the afternoon was an eternity. He smoked constantly, using three pipes in rotation so that the first had cooled by the time he finished the third. He had a great deal of work to do, work that had piled up on him while he had been immersed in the Cobb case: wills to draw, deeds to examine, letters to write, both friendly and professional. But he could not concentrate on any of it and finally gave up trying.

He stood at his window and looked down into the street; he paced from one end of the room to the other, laying a great cloud of smoke behind him.

He saw Mrs. Chute leave the bank in a hurry, reminding Drews of a frigate traveling in a high wind under heavy sail, with a mission to perform. He saw Alexander Whipple return to his print shop, walking as jauntily as ever, hiding the fear that Drews was certain was still in the little man. Then he saw Fred Bentley leave the jail and step into the Stockman's Bar. Within a minute or two he slammed out of the saloon and strode into the hotel.

Janice was right, Drews told himself. She knew men, at least the Bentley kind, who measured success in terms of the women they had possessed. The thought of Bentley even as much as laying his fat hands on Janice filled Drews with a crazy rage that was utterly unlike him. He never had had any respect for Bentley. Now he hated him. He whirled toward his desk, took a revolver from a drawer, checked it, and dropped it into his pocket.

He started toward the door, then stopped and walked to the window. To break in on Janice and Bentley would be the worst mistake he could make. He would ruin the trap she was setting for Bentley.

Drews had no hopes of her learning anything they didn't already know, but he had to let her try. Al Cobb's life was not worth so high a price, but that was Drews's way of looking at it, not Janice's. He was not entirely sure of her motives. Perhaps she thought she loved Cobb. She had said she wished she'd married him instead of Purvis. Or perhaps she felt she owed him a debt because he had brought Jerry back to her. Or it might be something else, the missing part of the relationship between Janice, and Cobb, and Purvis, that Drews had not yet learned.

Janice wanted him outside in the hall when she talked to Bentley, so he could be a witness to what the sheriff said. She had also told him to wait in his office until she sent for him. But how could she send for him? Maybe he should go to her. He couldn't go on waiting here.

Still he hesitated. Bentley would not stay with her very long now. Not in the daytime. It was too dangerous. He was a coward at times. He wanted Janice, but he was afraid of his wife and he was afraid of Purvis, so he would wait and return sometime during the night. At least that was the way Drews thought it would be. When he saw Bentley leave the hotel a few minutes later, he was convinced he was right.

Drews sat down at his desk, trying to decide what he should do. He suspected that Janice hadn't thought it through. She wouldn't have any means of getting a message to him without coming herself, and he doubted that she would risk that. She was too much in the public eye now. He had better go to her, he thought.

The hotel had a back stairs that led down to the alley. With any kind of luck, he could climb those stairs and get into Janice's room without being seen. The problem was finding out which room she had. Then he thought of a plan that might work. He rose, stuffing a pipe and tobacco can into his coat pocket, and promptly sat down again. His office door had opened and Ronald Purvis had come in.

"How are you, Drews?" the banker said as he closed the door.

"I'm fine, Purvis," Drews said. "And you?"

"I have no complaints concerning my health," Purvis said. "I do have business worries. That's why I'm here."

Purvis sat down in a rawhide-bottom chair across the desk from Drews, carefully placed his hat on his lap, and folded his hands. This was the last thing Drews had expected. The banker had never been in his office during the four years he had lived in Dead Horse, and for him to come now, of all days, seemed beyond explanation.

For a time Purvis said nothing, his pale-green eyes studying Drews with such cold intensity that Drews began to fidget. He felt as if he were some kind of strange bug that Purvis had placed under a microscope. Purvis's thin face seemed normal, and that surprised Drews after hearing Whipple tell how it had turned violently red when he had threatened the editor's life. The banker had complete control of himself, showing no nervousness whatever.

Still, something was missing in the man. Drews was reminded of the stories he had read of mad scientists who produced creatures capable of acting like human beings, but having no soul. Perhaps Ronald Purvis had not been born of woman.

If it had been a less serious moment, Drews would

have laughed at such a weird notion. Then, intuitively, he recognized what was missing in Purvis. The man had no mercy, no compassion; he sat there making as cold an appraisal of Drews as if he were a machine.

"I have heard enough about you, Drews," Purvis said finally, "to be sure that you are a capable lawyer. What I have in mind has nothing to do with criminal law, but it is to your credit that you made a valiant effort defending Cobb. You may have heard that I practiced law in Colorado, for a number of years, before I came here and bought the bank. I could handle this myself, but I find that the bank demands so much of my time that it is advisable to hire legal help."

Purvis paused, his eyes narrowing slightly. "You have, of course, read in the *Bugle* about the irrigation project we are working on. I am prepared to offer you $1,000 as a retainer to handle all the legal work that is necessary to make this project a going concern. Later you will be placed on a regular salary. I believe there is enough work to take all of your time. For the next few months, you will complete purchasing the land we need. Later, if there are any lawsuits, you will, of course, defend us in court. I have only one stipulation. You will have to drop your criminal cases."

"Beginning now?" Drews asked softly.

"Now."

"Including the Cobb case?"

"Yes."

It was bribery, slightly disguised, but bribery none the less. Purvis would pay the retainer, then fire him at high noon tomorrow, the instant Al Cobb was pronounced dead. Drews shook his head. "It's a tempting offer, but I'll have to turn it down."

There was not the slightest hint of emotion on Purvis's narrow face. He said, "Very well. I won't urge you, but I will tell you that you'll find it difficult to live in Dead Horse after this. Obviously you are turning me down because of the Cobb case. As you have no doubt heard, my wife has left me. She'll come back. I'll see that she does. I'm mentioning this because she told me you were still trying to free Cobb. As his lawyer that is your right, perhaps even your duty. But it does not involve seeing my wife, which I assume you have been doing or she wouldn't know about your efforts. I'm warning you. Stay away from her."

Purvis rose, his cold eyes not leaving Drews's face for an instant. A sudden chill ran down Drews's spine. He wondered why he had ever considered Purvis a weak man. He was capable of murdering in cold blood if it served his purpose, and now for the first time Drews fully understood the terror that had so completely demoralized Alexander Whipple.

Purvis walked to the door. Drews scooted his chair back, and lifting his gun from his pocket, laid it on the desk. He said, "Purvis, I have a gun. If you try to draw yours and threaten to kill me the way you did Whipple, I'll kill you. I want you to answer the question that turned you into a crazy man. Why do you hate Cobb?"

Purvis had turned and was facing Drews again. Now he laughed. He was not a laughing man, and his laughter was a strange sound, completely without mirth as it was. He said, "I'll tell you, although I don't like the term you used. I did not become a crazy man. I just lost my temper. I refuse to be questioned by a pipsqueak, and I think you will agree that is exactly what Whipple is. I have done a great deal for him. Now I'm going to break him.

"But to answer your question. As you know, I grew up with Al Cobb. He was a bad boy. He has lived exactly the kind of life that anyone who knew him then could have foreseen he would live. His hanging is long overdue. To release him would be to turn a mad dog loose upon society. If you, by some legal maneuver, are able to secure his release, you will endanger many lives. At best it would be a travesty of justice."

"There is nothing personal in your feeling about him?"

"Personal, in the way that I'm afraid of him just as I'm afraid of any killer."

"But he brought your boy back."

"On the contrary. He stole the child. Apparently he made contact with my wife, who paid him for the boy. She will not admit it, but that must have been what happened. It was sheer luck that put Fred Bentley where he was at the time Cobb delivered the child. He saw what had happened, so he did what any law man would have done."

Purvis turned, opened the door, and went out. Drews relaxed in his chair, sucking in a long breath of relief. He rose, and going to the window, watched Purvis cross the street to the bank. Drews picked up his hat, dropping his revolver into his pocket, and left his office.

He went directly to the hotel. Seeing that the lobby was empty, he crossed to the desk, and giving the register a quick turn, noted that Janice had Room 12. He whirled the book back, and was standing there as if waiting when Harvey Pearson appeared in the dining room doorway.

"Howdy, Linc," Pearson said. "You looking for a room?"

"No. I want you to prepare a good supper. Something special. Take it to Al Cobb this evening. What will it cost?"

"One dollar," Pearson said. "Given up on that bastard, and seeing that he gets a good meal the night before the hanging? That it?"

"I haven't given up." Drews laid a silver dollar on the desk. "He asked for a decent meal and I promised him he'd have it."

"All right, I'll see to it," Pearson said. "Be a big day tomorrow. A lot of folks ain't never seen a hanging, so we'll have a crowd."

Drews wheeled and strode out, anger beating at him so that he found it hard to control himself. He could not understand how any human being could be so callous about the taking of a human life, legal or otherwise, yet he knew that nearly everyone on Main Street felt the way Harvey Pearson did.

Drews circled the hotel, saw that no one was in the alley, and quickly climbed the stairs. The hall was empty. For once, he thought, luck was playing his way. Not that it made any real difference. He wasn't afraid of Purvis that much, but it might upset Janice's plan if Bentley heard that other men were calling on her.

Room 12 was the back corner one on his right. He

tapped on the door. She called, "Come in." He opened the door and stepped quickly inside, closing the door behind him. She had been standing by the window. She turned, her face brightening when she saw who it was. "I'm glad you came, Lincoln," she said. "Did anyone see you?"

"I don't think so. I came up the back stairs."

She nodded, pleased. "Good. I didn't think far enough ahead when I talked to you after dinner and said you'd hear from me. I just didn't think that I had no way of getting a message to you. I didn't want to go to your office. I don't want Bentley to know I'm even talking to another man."

"He was here to see you, wasn't he? I saw him come into the hotel and leave a few minutes later."

She smiled at the memory. "Yes, he was here. He's such a fool, Lincoln. He thinks no woman can resist him. He pretended to question me about what you were doing to free Al. That's the reason he gave Harvey Pearson for wanting to see me. I played helpless, and said I couldn't stand living with Ronnie and having him treat me the way he does, and I'd always admired Bentley and I knew how strong he was.

"His head got bigger and bigger, the more I talked. I said maybe we could have supper together, then he got cautious. He said people might not understand, meaning his wife, I suppose. He wanted me to take the next stage to Rawlins, and he'd visit me there. I pretended to think that was a good idea. Then he said he always takes a turn around town about midnight. Nobody would think anything of it if they saw him on the street. He'll come to see me then and I said I'd be expecting him."

"I don't like it," Drews said. "It won't work because he won't incriminate himself. Even if it does, it's too high a price for you to pay."

She shook her head. "No price except losing Jerry is too high. I suppose you'll have to hide somewhere until you see him come into my room, then be sure you're just outside."

"I'll be there," Drews promised.

"There's one more thing I want you to do. Go to the Stockman's Bar and get me the best bottle of whisky they have. Not the kind they put out for ordinary cow hands to drink, but the brand they'd give Ronnie if he went in with an important visitor."

"All right, I'll get it for you, but I'd better wait until dark." He turned toward the door, then a thought occurred to him that frightened him. He swung back to face her, asking, "Janice, is your husband capable of killing a person?"

She was startled by the question, then said, "Yes, he is. He tried to kill me once. He did kill a man when we lived in Fortune."

"I'm not surprised." Drews took the revolver out of his pocket and gave it to her. "I didn't think of that possibility until just now. He's a man who can't face losing anything he wants, is he?"

"That's right," she said. "He hates me, but still he won't let me go."

"Be careful," he warned. "Don't be afraid to use the gun if you have to, on him or Bentley."

"I won't," she said.

He motioned toward the door. "Better look outside."

She opened the door, glanced up and down the hall, and nodded. "It's safe," she said.

He left quickly and reached the stairs without anyone appearing in the hall. He found Whipple waiting in his office. "I was afraid you'd gone home," Whipple said.

"I'm ready to go now," Drews said. "Better come by my house about eleven. Maybe a little sooner. Bentley's visiting Mrs. Purvis after midnight. We'll have to find a vacant room and hide until Bentley shows up."

Whipple hesitated, fear having its way with him again, then he sighed. "Linc, this is too tough a game for me, but I'll be there."

"Don't tell your wife or anybody else," Drews warned. "Purvis would kill me, or you, or both of us, if he knew what we're up to. Bentley too, maybe. I wouldn't have said that a few hours ago, but I do now and I mean it."

"Not a word," Whipple promised. "I'm scared enough the way it is."

After he left, Drews glanced at his watch. Five o'clock! Cobb had 19 hours of life left. Drews wondered if he was counting the hours, too. But there was a difference. For Lincoln Drews the hours would be long; for Al Cobb they would be all too short.

CHAPTER XIV

FRED BENTLEY appeared in the corridor in front of Al Cobb's cell shortly after six, a plate of food in one hand, a cup of coffee in the other. He was chewing on a toothpick, and now he tipped it up at a rakish angle as he said affably, "Chow time, Killer."

Cobb had been looking forward to a good meal all afternoon. It was the only thing he had to look forward to. He'd had nothing to eat since breakfast, and he was hungry. Linc Drews had never broken a promise he'd made, and Cobb didn't expect him to now.

Cobb rose and walked toward Bentley. When he reached the cell door and could see the contents of the tin plate, he discovered it was the same kind of food he'd been getting ever since he'd been arrested. He wheeled and returned to his bunk, sick with disappointment. He'd go without anything to eat, if this was the best he could get. Drews must have forgotten all about it.

"Hey, don't you want it?" Bentley asked.

"Get to hell out of here," Cobb shouted. "If I get hold of that plate, I'll give it to you right in your mug."

"All right, all right," Bentley said. "You don't need to get sore. I don't know what you expect. I asked you at noon if you wanted something special and you didn't say, so I'm fetching your regular supper."

He turned as if to go back to his office, then stopped and looked back over his shoulder. "I don't blame you for not liking this grub. It ain't cooked like the food Harvey Pearson sets on the table in his dining room. He brought the best damned supper over while ago you ever seen. Fried chicken. Brown gravy. Mashed potatoes. Biscuits. Coffee. A big slab of apple pie. Perfect. Absolutely perfect."

Cobb jumped up and crossed the cell to the bars. "That's my supper. Give it to me."

"Yours?" Bentley said as if vastly surprised. "How do

you know it's yours?"

"Linc Drews said he'd see I had a good supper. Come on, give it to me."

"Well now, Killer, I can't do that," Bentley said. "You see, I didn't know it was for you. Like I said a minute ago, I figured you'd want your regular supper, since you didn't say nothing else to me at noon."

"Why can't you give it to me?"

Bentley shifted his toothpick. "Why, I thought Harvey fetched that meal for me, so I et it." He walked down the corridor to his office, laughing.

"You bastard," Cobb yelled at his back. "You God-damned, sneaking son of a bitch. You knew . . ."

Bentley slammed the metal door at the end of the corridor. Cobb gripped the bars of his cell, his knuckles white with the pressure. What was the use? Men like Ronnie Purvis and Fred Bentley ran the world, Ronnie doing the scheming, Bentley the dirty work. Cobb returned to his bunk and sat down, holding his head in his hands. His stomach ached with emptiness. He wondered if he'd have enough strength to climb the thirteen steps tomorrow noon.

Bentley returned, still chewing on the toothpick. He said, "It's after six, Killer. If I'm figuring right, you've got a little less'n eighteen hours of living to do. I've always wondered what a man thinks about when he gets that close to the end of his string."

When Cobb said nothing, Bentley went on, "Hanging is sure a hell of a way to die. It ain't so bad if the trap works right and you get your neck snapped, but if you don't, you swing back and forth till you choke to death, slow like."

This kind of torture was not part of the sentence Judge Charnley had given Cobb, but he knew there was nothing he could do about it, that Bentley was trying to goad him into an outbreak, and that then he'd laugh in his face.

A grin tugged at the corners of Bentley's heavy-lipped mouth and worked its way up into his face. "I guess you ain't heard the big news, kind of being out o' circulation like you are. Well sir, Ronald Purvis lost his wife. She moved into the hotel after going into the bank, and telling him right in front of Augie Nolan and Mrs. Chute that she was leaving him. Now why do you suppose she'd do a thing like that?"

Cobb hadn't intended to give Bentley the satisfaction of letting him know he was listening, but his head snapped up when Bentley said Ronald Purvis had lost his wife. He couldn't help it. He looked away quickly, refusing to ask the questions that prodded his mind. He saw the wickedness in Bentley's face and sensed that this was only the beginning.

"I reckon you knew Mrs. Purvis, didn't you, Killer?" Bentley went on. "I been kind o' curious about how well you knew her. The talk around town says you and her and Ronald growed up together somewhere in Nebraska. Now it appears she's real interested in you. She says to Ronald, there in the bank, that Linc Drews is gonna get you off and there's nothing Ronald can do about it. I wonder why she'd give a good, thin damn about a bastard like you. She's a fine lady, Mrs. Purvis is."

Cobb's hands rested on his knees. He stared at the

floor, breathing hard, but still refusing to let Bentley see the torment that was in him.

"Well sir, maybe you knowed her purty damned well when you was a kid," Bentley went on. "But the bad men always wind up dancing on nothing and looking at the sky, and the good men like me get the cream. I'd call Mrs. Purvis the cream, all right. She needs a man. She told me that and I'd say she's a good judge of men. She figures that I can give her something she ain't been getting real regular. I seen her this afternoon in her hotel room. Maybe I'll have a little visit with her again, maybe tonight when I go around town seeing if everything's buttoned up fit and proper."

Bentley was standing close to the bars. Cobb tried to hold back, tried to tell himself that Bentley was only guessing about him and Janice, guessing because Janice had been foolish enough to show her concern by saying publicly that Linc Drews would get him off. Then his self-control broke and he lunged forward off his bunk, a fist driving between the bars at Bentley's leering face. But the sheriff was poised, expecting this. He jumped back and leaned against the bars on the opposite side of the corridor, laughing so hard that tears ran down his face.

"Don't touch her, Bentley," Cobb said, his voice shaking. "If you do, I'll kill you. By God, that's a promise."

"Kill me?" Bentley chortled. "What are you fixing to use for a weapon? A mean look, maybe? I'm too tough to be rubbed out that way, Killer. I tell you I'm a hell of a good man and Mrs. Purvis knows it. She's the kind of woman who gets under your hide, don't she? Well, I've been waiting for this. When she first got to town, I let her know how it was with me. Took her a while to think it over, but she finally came to it. I reckon it'll be worth the waiting."

He straightened, jamming his hands deep into his pockets. He said scornfully, "I don't know why a son of a bitch like you ever figured you had any chance with a woman like her. You ain't fit to kiss her ass, let alone anything else."

Bentley had had his fun and now he was tired of it. He walked down the corridor, swaggering a little, and went into his office, shutting the metal door behind him.

Tears of frustration and rage poured down Cobb's face. He sprawled on his bunk, fists beating at the hard surface. Bentley didn't know; he couldn't know how it had been. Janice wouldn't have any part of a man like him. He'd find it out soon enough. But Bentley was right about one thing: Al Cobb wasn't the man for her, either, not even if by some miracle Linc Drews succeeded in freeing him.

There had been a time when it might have been different, if life hadn't dealt the cards the way it had. He hadn't done many honorable things in his life, but he had done one once that he had regretted ever since. The world was made for hypocrites like Ronnie Purvis, who saw no virtue in being honorable, only in the appearance of honor.

But there had been this one time in Fortune, Colorado . . . the one time that gave him his most treasured memory. He thought about it now, and he forgot his hunger and the 13 steps he must climb tomorrow, and the fact that life would end for him in a few hours. He relaxed, all of it coming back almost as clearly and sharply as the day it had happened.

CHAPTER XV

A L COBB had spent two years carrying a marshal's star in Nevada mining towns. Without thinking much about it, he had supposed that Fortune would be like them, sprawled out on a sagebrush flat or along the bottom of a sun-baked gulch where it got hotter than the hinges of hell. But it wasn't. Fortune, in the high country of the San Juans, might have been in a different world.

He had climbed for miles. He had left Montrose the morning before and had followed the Uncompahgre River, the hills closing in, the valley steadily narrowing. He had spent the night in Ouray where the mountains had been all around him, great peaks that reached for the sky. He had stared at them, at the mines above timber line where men had tunneled into the mountains in their eternal search for wealth; and he had marveled how machinery and heavy timbers had ever reached those high peaks on the backs of tiny burros.

A hell of a way to make a dollar. Butch Cassidy's method had been simpler. The day of using a six-gun to take money from those who could spare it was gone, but there were those who lived down here in the comforts of town who had the same general idea: the saloon keepers, the gamblers, the con men, the pimps and the whores.

Yes, and the big wheelers and dealers like Ronnie Purvis. In the morning when he had ridden on, he'd had every intention of killing Ronnie. It would be nothing more than delayed justice.

He reached Fortune early in the afternoon, following a shelf road carved out of the side of a canyon wall. The canyon was no more than a narrow slit in the earth's surface, the pounding river a silver cord far below him. Now, looking at the camp, he would have said it was impossible to build it here, if he wasn't seeing it with his own eyes.

Business buildings flanked the narrow street. On one side the back ends of the structures rose directly over the deep canyon; on the other side the buildings were crowded between the street and the slope that lifted sharply toward the sky. Up there on the mountain, above Main Street, men had somehow contrived to build cabins among the spruce and aspen. Across the canyon, the peaks rose so sharply and so high that even now the sun did not touch Main Street.

He left his horse in a livery stable, took a room in a hotel, shaved, put on a clean shirt, and set out to find Ronnie Purvis. And maybe to see Janice. He wanted to see her, and yet he didn't. He had wondered about her, of course. She'd be changed, a woman now instead of a girl. Would she be beautiful, as he remembered her? Or had time and distance exaggerated her beauty in the mental picture he had retained?

Maybe she was fat and dowdy, her figure destroyed by childbearing. He would duck out of sight, if he saw her coming down the street with six children hanging to her skirt and a baby in her arms. Maybe he'd duck, anyhow. He wasn't sure whether he wanted her to know he was here. Even in his wildest daydreams, he had never seriously imagined there could be any future for them. Better do what he came for and get out of camp and forget her.

He walked up one side of the street to the big stamp mill at the upper end that made the air hideous with its continual hammering, and came down the other side. For a small camp Fortune was a boisterous, busy place, the street congested with traffic: ore wagons, burro trains, buggies and rigs of all kinds. Even the boardwalks were crowded, mostly by miners, and he realized suddenly that he was conspicuous, that he was probably the only man in town who looked like a cow hand.

If he met Ronnie on the street, he'd hurry on by, confident that Ronnie would not recognize him. He was heavier than he had been the last time Ronnie had seen him, and he had grown a sweeping yellow mustache. His clothes were different, too. Besides, and this was important, he was expecting to see Ronnie, but Ronnie wasn't expecting to see him.

He completed his quick inspection of the town, discovering there was only one first-class saloon, the Silver Palace. He went in, took a quick look around, then shouldered through the crowd to the far end of the bar. He ordered a drink and stood there, watching the door. He'd know Ronnie the instant he saw him. He was sure of that.

No miners were in the saloon, which was exactly what Cobb had expected. Some of the men undoubtedly were associated with mining—bookkeepers, superintendents, and other office workers and executives—but he had a hunch that most of these men were bankers, lawyers, or businessmen.

Certainly the Silver Palace catered to the carriage trade. The big back bar mirror, the polished cherry-wood bar, the expensive chandelier hanging from the center of the ceiling: all testified to that. It was Ronnie Purvis's kind of place, where the big dealers and wheelers would gather to make their deals. Sooner or later Ronnie would show up. He did, just after six o'clock.

Ronnie walked directly to the bar and ordered a drink. He had the look of money about him, of big money. He wasn't much heavier than Cobb remembered him, his face still narrow, his features sharp. But he had matured, having lost the adolescent gawkiness that his height and skinny body had given him. He was clad in a black broadcloth suit which undoubtedly had been tailored for him. He wore a diamond stickpin, a watch chain from which dangled an elk-tooth charm, and he carried a heavy, gold-headed cane which he leaned against the bar when he reached for his drink.

Within a matter of minutes, men gathered around him. It was no proof of popularity, Cobb thought, but more likely proof that he had money. There would always be those who hoped to shake some of it loose and have it drop into their pockets. The odds were that it would work the other way.

Some of the men who were hanging on every word Ronnie spoke were probably Easterners who had come west in search of the quick dollar. Cobb had seen them in Nevada many times. They acted as if they were stupid sheep wanting to be sheared, and Cobb had no doubt that Ronnie carried a pair of sharp shears in his pocket.

Watching him, Cobb realized that Ronnie had changed far more than his initial inspection indicated. He removed his pince-nez glasses, he rubbed the bridge of his nose thoughtfully, gestured with his right hand which still held the glasses, and then replaced them.

Somehow Ronnie Purvis had achieved a cool dignity which automatically raised him above the average human level of the room. Maybe the others sensed his superiority and snobbishness, but they recognized his business acumen, too. Maybe they hated him even while they fawned over him, Cobb told himself cynically. But there wasn't a man in the lot who wouldn't climb up to Ronnie's level if he could.

Cobb motioned to the bartender who was the closest to him. "Who's the tall gent at the other end of the bar?" he asked.

"Ronald Purvis," the bartender said. "He's the richest man in camp, I guess. Buys and sells mines, and damned if he wasn't born lucky. They say he makes a profit every time."

"He looks like a lawyer," Cobb said as if guessing.

"He is," the bartender said. "Best lawyer in camp, they claim. Ain't lost more'n two, three cases since he got here, but the talk is he makes most of his money from dealing in mines."

"And never touched a pick handle," Cobb said.

"No, by God, he never did," the barman agreed sourly. "But he's tough with that cane he carries. Several times men who claim he cheated 'em have jumped him, and he just beats hell out of 'em with that cane."

"Another Bat Masterson."

"You know Bat?"

"No. Just heard about him."

"Well, I knew Bat in Creede," the bartender said. "All the talk about him using his cane is a bunch of crap, but not with Purvis. I've seen him do it."

"Can he handle a gun?"

"Yeah, in his way. He's a tough bastard, even if he don't look it. He carries a short-barreled revolver in his coat pocket. I seen a man try to draw on him, and he shot the fellow right from the pocket. Got him in the guts, too."

Ronnie was leaving now, a couple of men following him to the door. Cobb paid for his drink and worked his way toward the street, wanting to follow Ronnie but not too close. The light was thin when he reached the street, the mountains to the west straining out most of the evening sunlight. Cobb remained a safe distance behind Ronnie, as he turned up a side street and climbed its looping length to a white frame house, one of the few in camp.

No luxury here, Cobb thought, and was surprised. Then it occurred to him that Fortune was not the place where Ronnie would make a show of his wealth. He would pile up his money, and when he had what he considered enough, he'd sell out here and move on to Denver or Colorado Springs. There he'd continue his law practice and build a fine house where it would mean something. Maybe become a banker or a broker. Or a judge. Go into politics maybe. The world was made for men like Ronnie Purvis, Cobb told himself, as he had so many times.

He stood across the street from Ronnie's house, in a growth of aspens, and watched. Ronnie sat down and began to read a newspaper. No sign of children, and Cobb was surprised at that, too. For some reason he had thought of Janice as being a mother; but now it occurred to him that Ronnie was the last man in the world who would willingly become a father.

Then Cobb's heart gave a great leap. Janice came out of the kitchen, and he saw her clearly with the lamp light upon her face. He had not exaggerated her beauty in the mental picture he had retained of her. If anything, he had forgotten and had not done her justice. Or maybe the years had brought a ripe, mature beauty to her that made her far more attractive than the girl he had seen briefly on her porch in Royal.

He doubted that she had gained a pound in the eight years since he had seen her. Her figure was as trim as it had been as a girl. When she turned and walked back into the kitchen, she moved with the same titillating grace that had so excited him in school when he had followed her down the hall.

Ronnie rose and, moving to the windows, pulled down the green shades. Cobb walked back to the hotel, all the old desire for Janice boiling up in him again. He had supper and went to his room. He sat down on his bed and thought about it.

Shooting Ronnie was too quick, too good. He should suffer, just as he had made Al Cobb suffer. There was a difficulty, too, that Cobb had not fully considered. Ronnie was not a man to face him and draw a gun and make a fair fight out of it. The only way Cobb could kill him was to cut him down in cold blood, and he wasn't a man who could do that.

No, killing Ronnie Purvis wasn't the way. Cobb would have Janice; he would possess her with all the brutal passion that the years had stored up in him. He didn't care what happened to him after that. He would have his revenge upon the two people he hated, the people who had given him three years in the reform school and sent him out of Royal on a freight train, crazy with fear of what would happen to him if they caught him after killing the banker's son.

They would both live with the shame of it. He had told her once he was a better man than Ronnie. Tomorrow she would know, and Ronnie would know that she knew, and nothing would ever be the same for them again.

He had breakfast in the morning, idling away the early hours because he wanted to give Ronnie plenty of time to get out of the house. He circled it so he would be above it, walking briskly in the sharp morning air that was pungent with the smell of aspen smoke that rose from the chimney of every cabin in Fortune.

He stopped directly above the Purvis house and stood there, watching, surprised at something he had not noticed the evening before in the thinning light. A log barn stood up the hill from the house, and there was a new, red-wheeled buggy in the yard between the barn and the house.

She came out of the back door of the house and walked

in her quick-stepping, graceful way to the barn. He moved swiftly downslope from the aspens, where he had been standing, to the barn, and went in through the door she had left open. This time, he told himself, there would be no father to break the door down, no Royal marshal, no old man Goslin.

She was standing with her back to the door currying a bay gelding, unaware that he had come in until he stood a step from her and said, "Hello, Janice."

She whirled, crying out. He had intended to slap a hand over her mouth to keep her from making a sound, but he was too slow. She recognized him at once. She whispered, "Al." He put out a hand, but he didn't drive the palm against her mouth. He realized she wasn't going to scream; he saw an expression sweep across her face that he had never dreamed he would see: an expression of joy and eagerness that erased the hate for her, and told him he could not do what he had planned.

She dropped the brush and currycomb into the straw and threw herself into his arms. She whispered, "Oh Al, Al," and hugged him, her mouth on his. For a time they held each other that way, her lips and her arms all telling him she had waited too long for this moment.

Finally she drew back and stood looking at him, shaking her head and smiling a little as she murmured, "What a man you've become, Al. I've wondered so many times how you'd look."

She picked up the brush and currycomb and set them on the shelf, then she pulled the door shut and dropped the hook into the staple. Watching her, he thought that she, too, was remembering Gillette's barn and what had happened so many years ago.

She took his hand and led him to the pile of hay in the back of the barn. She said, "This time Ronnie won't tell the marshal about us. He's gone to Ouray for the day." She looked at him as if trying to read his mind. "You didn't know about that, did you?"

He shook his head. "No, I didn't know." So it had been his fault. If he hadn't warned Ronnie to stay away from Gillette's barn, it wouldn't have happened.

She sat down, tugging on his arm until he dropped down beside her. She said, "I can only ask you to forgive me for what I said that night. I can't undo what's been done. I was afraid and I got panicky, and I said what I did before I thought what it would do to you. Afterwards I went to the marshal and told old man Goslin, but they wouldn't listen. They didn't believe me. They thought I was just feeling sorry for you. I tried, Al. I tried the best I could."

He stared at her, wanting to believe her, but he couldn't. He said, "There was another time. You told me I'd killed Ronnie."

"I didn't lie that time," she said quickly. "I thought he was dead. I couldn't find his pulse. But even if I'd known he was alive, I would have done exactly what I did. You had to run while there was time. Don't you see? They'd have put you in jail again because you'd hit him. Don't you know that?"

"Yes, I guess I should," he said against his will, knowing he had hated her all this time for no good reason. The world was made for Ronnie Purvis, and the town of Royal most of all.

"If you'd only written to me," she said. "I'd have gone to you. Anywhere, anytime. I looked for a letter from you for so long, but it never came."

"You married Ronnie," he said accusingly.

"Yes," she said. "Don't ask me why. There just didn't seem to be anything else to do when I didn't hear from you."

So that had been his fault, too. But he couldn't have taken her with him, riding as he had with Texas Slim and hiding out in Brown's Hole, and after that the years of drifting. He shook his head. "I guess it's better the way it turned out. I couldn't have given you what he has."

"Better?" she cried. "You don't know how it's been, Al. You're right about not giving me what he has. You wouldn't if you could. You're decent and you're honest. I knew that when we were kids, but not the way I know it now."

Her lips were very close to his. He kissed her, and then the barriers were down and the earth and the heavens shook for them. Afterwards as she lay in his arms, she said, "It's not too late. Take me with you."

"I can't," he said miserably. "I never dreamed it would be this way. I'm broke. I can't take care of you. I've made money and I've thrown it away. I just never knew."

"If you've made it," she said, "you can make it again."

"I need a little time," he said. "Stay here until I can send for you and take care of you." He kissed her, and the need for each other rose in them again.

He rode out of Fortune that afternoon. If it had been a few years ago, he thought, he would have made the money quickly, Cassidy style. But only a fool would try it now. So he rode north into Wyoming where a range war was boiling up in the Big Elk country.

He hired out for fighting wages, not knowing or caring much about the right or wrong of it, but wanting to make the big money quickly. Three men from the other side jumped him in town one afternoon. He took them, all three, and in thirty seconds made his reputation as a bad man.

The war wasn't over and he stayed on because they needed him, still making big money. She wrote him that they had moved to Dead Horse, then in the late winter she wrote that she'd had a baby, a boy, and that she had named him Jerry.

After that he quit writing. He had saved his money and he had enough for the two of them to make a start somewhere, but not enough for three that included a small baby. Now she would not leave the security Ronnie could give them.

That night he got drunk. Then he sat in on a poker game and lost $300. After that, he grew bitter and silent and withdrawn, for he could not forget what might have been and now would never be, and how much of the fault was his.

CHAPTER XVI

JANICE looked at her watch and saw that it was supper time, but she wasn't hungry. She hated the thought of going downstairs to the dining room, and being stared at by everyone who had heard. And of course by now everyone in town had heard. But she had gone this far; she could not back out of the bargain she had made with herself and Lincoln Drews. Let these people have their look and their gossip. She thought with a sort of perverse pride that even their wildest flights of imagination would be short of the truth.

She stood in front of her mirror, at seven, and pinned up her hair. She put on her hat and straightened her skirt and went downstairs. The dining room was crowded, but she found a table in a corner and picked up a soup-splattered menu.

She felt the eyes of everyone in the room staring at her: Doc Chute and his wife. The Frank McClains. Some businessmen who were eating alone. Two cowmen from the upper Dead Horse. Several drummers whose names she did not know.

A buzz swept over the dining room, then everyone seemed to be trying to look the other way. She studied the menu until she made her choice, then sat looking out of the window, her hands folded, her reticule on her lap.

Presently Harvey Pearson came into the dining room from the kitchen, saw her, and coming to her, sat down at her table. Leaning forward, he said in a low tone, "Miz Purvis, your husband wants you to come home."

"I'm not going home, Harvey," she said.

He squirmed in his chair, his round face turning pink. He said, "Miz Purvis, I'm kind o' backed into a corner. Your husband don't want me to let you stay the night here. He said to make you come home where you belong."

She looked at him scornfully. "Is Lincoln Drews the

only man in this town who isn't a coward? Do you all get down on your knees in front of my husband every time he snaps his fingers? Well, Harvey, I've got on my knees in front of him for the last time. I've left him and I'm not going back. If you want to throw me out into the street, you'll have to do it. Perhaps I can find a woodshed to sleep in tonight."

"No ma'am, I won't do that," he said heavily. He looked around for a waitress, saw one, and beckoned to her, calling, "Miz Purvis is ready to order now."

Pearson left the dining room as the waitress came to Janice's table. By eight o'clock she had finished her supper, but still she lingered over her coffee, not wanting to face the loneliness of her room. The dining room lamps had been lighted. Everyone was gone except her and the drummers. She did not feel quite so alone down here, then she realized it was almost dark and Lincoln Drews would be coming soon.

She finished her coffee and, picking up her reticule, left the dining room. The drummers turned to stare at her, their eyes frankly admiring and speculative. Most men looked at her that way; she had seen the same expression in Fred Bentley's eyes the first time they had met.

She never understood why men thought of her that way. She wasn't the kind of woman they judged her to be, but men thought of her that way and so did their wives. After all these years, it still bothered her, for she had never become used to it. Now that she had left Ronnie, she supposed that every man in town would try to get into bed with her. Every man but Lincoln Drews, if she had made the right appraisal of him. That was strange, too, because he was the only man in Dead Horse to whom she would give a second thought.

When she reached her room, she shut the door and took off her hat. She stood by the window looking out into the darkness, her thoughts somber. She was a little frightened, now that the time was close for Fred Bentley to come. He was an animal: the situation could easily get out of hand. But she would go through with it. She had been a coward once—that night in Gillette's barn. She had paid for that moment of weakness many times since then. She would not be a coward tonight.

It was nearly nine before she heard the tap on her door. She crossed the room and, opening it, saw that it was Lincoln Drews. She said in quick relief, "I'm glad it's you. Come in. I'll light a lamp. I was just standing here thinking about Al."

She lighted a lamp on her bureau. Drews closed the door and handed her the bottle of whisky. "The best from the Stockman's Bar," he said. "You'll have Bentley purring after a few drinks of this."

She smiled as she set the bottle on the bureau. "I hope he'll purr the right words." She looked at Drews and shook her head, her smile a forced one. "I'm scared, Lincoln. I'm awfully scared."

"I told you that you were paying too high a price," Drews said. "I'll see Bentley and tell him not to come."

"No, don't do that," she said quickly. "It's Al I'm scared about. What do we have, about 15 hours?" He nodded, and she asked, "What can we do in that time?"

"Nothing, maybe," he said.

"Suppose you can't make connections with the Governor," she asked. "I mean, if Bentley tells us what we have to know. Maybe the telephone wires are down. Or maybe he's gone and you can't contact him? Is there anything you can do?"

"Nothing," he said. "We've got to be lucky."

"I've been such a coward," she said bitterly. "I should have gone to you the day Charnley sentenced Al. Maybe there would have been time then. I just couldn't bring myself to do it. I kept thinking that something would happen to save him, and I wouldn't have to do anything. Then I woke up this morning and nothing had happened, so I knew I was the only one who could help him."

She sat down on the bed, weary with the feeling of defeat. She said, "I should have left Ronnie a long time ago, but I guess I've been a little afraid of him. Then after Jerry came, I thought I had to stay with Ronnie for the baby's sake. I didn't have any money and I wasn't trained for any kind of work. Now I'll be cut off with nothing and maybe I won't save Al's life, either."

"Purvis says Cobb stole the boy, and you paid him the ransom to get him back," Drews said.

"It's a lie," she said. "His whole life is a lie." She glanced at Drews. "Do you believe me? Somebody has to believe me."

"I believe you," he said gently, "but I'm not the problem."

"I know." She stared at her hands that were folded on her lap. "When I was a girl, I had everything I wanted. Almost everything. People thought I was a very good girl and never had a sinful thought or desire, but they were wrong. I just wasn't honest enough to tell anyone except Al. All of his troubles started because I wasn't honest about him. Lately, after what's happened, I've thought so much about honesty and justice and things like that." She looked up. "What's the worst sin of all, Lincoln? I don't mean what the preachers talk about, but the way you see it, as a lawyer. Or just as a human being?"

He was silent for a moment, his eyes probing her as if trying to determine what had brought this on. Finally he said, "Selfishness, I guess. Not the selfishness that all of us have more or less, but complete, self-centered selfishness."

"Yes," she murmured, "that's what I think. That's the sin Ronnie is guilty of all the time. He never once has thought of my welfare or happiness. He only wants a wife as an asset to his business and social life, just as his house is. Or the deer in the front yard. That's why he'll do all he can to make me come back to him. It's a mark against his position in the community because I left him. He always reacts the same way. To Jerry. To people who are his friends, and yet he is very smug in his belief that he is a paragon of virtue. I guess everyone in town thinks so, too."

"Almost everyone," Drews admitted.

She rose and walked around the room, a restlessness in her she could not control. She said, "I don't condone the things Al has done that are wrong. You said he was a hard man. I guess he is. I didn't talk to him much when he brought Jerry back, but I watched him at the trial and I felt a toughness about him he didn't used to have. But it's not his fault. Life hasn't been fair with him."

"Don't blame life, Janice," Drews said. "We all have a choice. Every one of us makes a choice every day."

But she would have no part of that kind of thinking. She hurried on, "I don't condone killing men, and I guess Al's been guilty of that. I don't condone stealing other men's property, and maybe he's guilty of that, too."

She paused, thinking she could add adultery to the list of Al's sins, but if she did, she must share his guilt. She had never permitted herself to think of it that way, though. She had never regretted it, either. She had considered it a sort of compensation for what she had done that time in Gillette's barn. Not that she could undo the wrong, but it was the only gesture she could make in that direction.

"What I'm trying to say is that Al has never made any claim to goodness," she went on hurriedly. "Ronnie has. He's a pillar of the church, of the lodge, of all the accepted standards of goodness in the community, yet he's caused men to kill themselves. He's taken their homes from them under the pretext that the bank cannot extend credit too far. Other respectable men, like Judge Charnley and Fred Bentley have schemed along with him, and I've stood by with the rest of the wives and kept still. This time I won't, Lincoln. I can't. For once, we've got to see that justice is done."

He walked to her and put his hands on her shoulders. He said, "Janice, you are a wonderful woman."

"No, no," she cried. "I'm not. I'm just trying to get something off my conscience."

"I'm not going to argue with you," he said gently.

"Condemn yourself if you must, but today I've learned to admire you for your courage. There is one thing you're going to have to start thinking about. Suppose we free Al Cobb and he wants you to go away with him? Then you'll have to make a choice."

He turned and left the room. She stood there a long time, staring at the door. Slowly she began to undress. She put on her nightgown and the lace negligee, and lay down on the bed to wait for Bentley. She wasn't frightened now. She could handle Bentley, drunk or sober. And Lincoln Drews would be outside her door.

She closed her eyes and thought about her years with Ronnie. Her first mistake was marrying him, but her second mistake, and for this she had no excuse, was trying to make the best of a bad marriage. She should have left him a long time ago.

CHAPTER XVII

JANICE'S first years of marriage were not happy ones, but they were bearable. Ronnie was young, he was only beginning to feel his way as a practising lawyer, and because they lived for a time in Royal, he was overshadowed by his father. For all of these reasons, there was a trace of humility in him.

For Ronnie, life was stifling in Royal. He could not bear to be overshadowed by anyone, and that included his father. One evening he told Janice they were moving to Colorado. He didn't ask. He simply told her. First they went to Denver, but Ronnie didn't like it there. They took the narrow gauge over Marshal Pass to Montrose on the western slope. He explored several towns on the Uncompahgre and the Gunnison and the Grand, but none of them suited him. They were agricultural trading centers, too much like Royal.

They reversed direction and went into the San Juan mining country. Janice loved Ouray, but she didn't say so. When they settled down, it would be in a town Ronnie liked, not one that she did. They took the stage on up the Uncompahgre to Fortune. Ronnie stepped out, looked up and down Main Street, and when Janice stood beside him in the ankle-deep mud, he said, "This is it."

She never knew what Ronnie saw in Fortune, or why he immediately sensed that this was the place where he wanted to live. She didn't ask him. That was one of the first things she had learned not to do. Even if he had let her ask the question, she doubted that he could answer. Ordinarily he was not a man to give way to hunches, but that must have been what he did in this case. At least there was some secret affinity between him and this booming mining camp perched so precariously on the side of the mountain.

Ronnie never had any reason to regret his decision. He was an instant success as a lawyer. That did not surprise Janice, but she was surprised at his success as a buyer and seller of mines. He never told her how much money he made and again she never asked; but from some of the things he said to her, and the things she heard when they entertained other business leaders of the camp, she knew he was doing very well, indeed.

Janice was lonely; she found no one in Fortune that she really liked, but again life was tolerable. She had learned to live within herself in those first terrible months after Al Cobb had gone to the reform school; learned that she must accept life as it was, that it was the height of foolishness to dream of might-have-beens.

After her marriage she learned this simple truth all over again. It was a man's world, her physical needs of food, shelter, and clothing were being met. If she found the marriage bed less than satisfying, and even if she was to be denied the privilege of motherhood, she was still luckier than many women she knew.

Too, there were some physical features about Fortune that she liked. Just living there was a challenge. Every winter, snow hung on the high peaks above the camp like the sword of Damocles, and no one knew when he went to bed at night whether he would be alive in the morning. Many times Janice heard the thunder of avalanches roaring down the steep slopes; many times she heard tales of ore wagons and stage coaches, and even entire mining camps being swept away and buried under tons of snow. But Fortune lived a charmed life.

She loved the summers even though they were short; she liked to drive down to Ouray, or up some of the roads that twisted in great loops on the side of the mountain above Fortune. Ronnie did do one generous thing, but whether he did it for her or to show off his own prosperity was a question in her mind. He bought her an expensive buggy, a whip with silver ferrules on the handle, and a spirited bay gelding.

After that she was not dependent upon the livery stable when she wanted to take a drive. Ronnie was no hand with horses; he wanted nothing to do with the bay, so

Janice took care of him and he became to her a much beloved pet, in the way that a cat or dog does for some people.

Then Al Cobb came, and the world was turned upside down again for Janice. The might-have-been of years ago became a strong probability. Ronnie made no pretense of feeling any obligation toward making her happy. She was a housekeeper, someone to keep him warm during the cold winter nights, a social asset. No more. Although she had kept her marriage vows until Al came to her that morning in the log barn, she had no regret or feeling of guilt for breaking them. She would have gone anywhere with Al without feeling a single pang of conscience.

Ronnie, she told herself, could always hire someone to do for him as much as she had done. It was different with Al. He loved her and she loved him and he needed her. That was the difference between making life a joy or a tolerable existence. When she discovered she was pregnant, she felt like singing every waking moment of the day.

In less than a month from the time Al was in Fortune, Ronnie informed her he had bought the bank in Dead Horse, Wyoming, and they would move at once. She was never sure of his reasons. She often wondered if he had seen Al when he'd been in Fortune, or had somehow been informed of his presence. Or maybe he knew that he would never be more than one of several important men in Fortune; but in Dead Horse he would be Mr. Ronald Purvis, the banker, the giver and taker of credit, and therefore the giver and taker of life. In a small way he would be God, and that, she knew, was exactly what he wanted to be.

They made the move to Dead Horse, Ronnie built the big house and furnished it without asking Janice's advice on anything. He planned the landscaping, he bought the bronze deer, he had the iron fence built around his property. When she bought the Prang chromo and hung it in the parlor, the one bright spot in the funereal decorations of the room, he ignored it. She didn't press her luck. She sensed that if she hung anything else on the wall, he would jerk it down and throw it away.

When she told him about the baby, he accepted it as he accepted her presence in the house, accepted the fact that she breathed and slept and ate. During the latter months of her pregnancy she thought he was a little gentler, a little more thoughtful. Perhaps she imagined it. She wasn't sure, for if he did anything for her, he performed the act with a coldness and formality that killed what might have been with some other man a feeling of rapport.

All the time she was thinking of the might-have-been, the hoped-for letter from Al saying that she was to come to him. She had no feeling of hypocrisy, of sympathy for Ronnie because she planned to leave him. She had given him what he had wanted in a wife. She had served his purpose, nothing more. She would have gone to Al even during the last weeks, her body clumsy and swollen as it was. But the might-have-been never became anything else, the hoped-for letter never came.

When the baby arrived, he was round-faced with curly yellow hair. He was short and chunky, showing none of the long-boned slimness that characterized Ronnie. He stood beside her bed, Doc Chute and Maggie Nolan standing behind him. He looked at the baby and turned and walked away. She was never sure whether he knew or not, but within a matter of weeks she realized he hated the baby, perhaps only because the child was an intrusion in his way of life.

When she had her strength back, she wrote to Al that she had Jerry. She could not bring herself to say that this was his baby, that it was his duty to come and take care of them, or at least to write to her, asking her to come to him and promising he would look out for them. He would know, she thought. Then the letters from him which had been few and quite formal stopped coming entirely. After that she faced the bitter fact that the might-have-been would never be, that she had been a dreamer, and the baby was all she would ever have of Al Cobb.

The next three years were bearable only because of Jerry. Whatever trace of humility Ronnie had once had was gone. He was coldly courteous to her in front of Maggie Nolan and Lena Walker and their guests; but when they were alone, his little cruelties grew day by day until she knew she could not go on.

She did her best to meet the growing demands he made upon her, the parties and the suppers and the Sunday dinners. She constantly complimented him upon the way he handled things, his appearance, his position in the community. She hated herself for this hypocrisy, but it was the only way she could live with him at all. Even so, his greatest satisfaction in life came through putting a knife into her and twisting it, and watching her writhe under the pain of it.

Her cup overflowed one Saturday evening, after they had entertained the Charnleys and the Whipples at supper. She had done her best to be charming; she had given special attention to planning the meal and to her appearance; and she had thought the whole thing had gone off very well. When she was getting ready for bed he came into her room and dressed her down in his cold, impersonal way. The evening had been a failure, she looked like a hag, and her conversation had been even more boring than usual. He was not satisfied until she began to cry.

She said, "I can't stand this, Ronnie. I'm going to take Jerry and go away."

He stood over her, very tall and, to her, suddenly very sinister and threatening. He said, "I won't let you. I never give up anything that's mine."

He left and went to his own room. When she regained her composure, she looked in on Jerry and saw that he was asleep; then she returned to her room and wrote to Al. She wasn't sure he was still in the Big Elk country, but she hoped her letter would be forwarded. She was going to Rawlins from Dead Horse, she said, and told him where he could find her. She would remain in Dead Horse one more week. She wasn't sure she could go on living with Ronnie that long, but she would try. She begged him to meet her in Rawlins if he could, but whether he did or not, she had reached the place where she must leave Dead Horse.

Five days passed before his answer came. The letter was addressed to Lena Walker as she had asked him to do. Lena brought it directly to her. Al would be in

Rawlins when she got there. He was in the Big Horns working for a sheep outfit. It was a long way across Wyoming, but he was leaving immediately. She cried then. The might-have-been was still within her reach.

When the first moment of elation passed, she faced the reality of it. He had let four years pass without sending for her. He had not written for three. Certainly he did not feel toward her as she thought she felt toward him. Now it was not so much a case of going to him because she loved him, as it was a matter of getting away from a marriage which had become intolerable. She had to go; she could not stay.

She thought of the time between now and when she was to meet Al. It was a long way to Rawlins. There were only two stages a week, and the next one would not get there in time. She would have to hire a rig from Pete Walker. Hurriedly, she packed a bag with Jerry's things and started to pack hers.

She would leave right after dinner, telling Maggie and Lena she was taking Jerry for a ride. If she couldn't sneak the suitcase and bag out of the house without them seeing what she had, they would have to think what they wanted to. Ronnie was eating at the hotel with a politician from Cheyenne who was visiting in Dead Horse. She would be well on her way to Rawlins before he knew she was gone.

She had just finished putting the lid down on the suitcase and latching it when she heard Ronnie say in his cold, distant voice, "What are you doing?"

She whirled to face him. "I thought you were eating in the hotel today."

"Later. I asked you what you were doing."

He knew, she thought, regardless of the lie she gave him, so she might as well tell the truth. She said, "I'm leaving you. I told you last night."

"And I told you I never gave up anything that was mine," he said. "What do you think Fred Bentley and the Judge and the rest of them would say? Do you think for a minute I'll let you make me the laughing stock of the town?"

"You can find another woman."

"I don't intend to. In some ways you are desirable. Other men think you are." He shook his narrow head, his mouth so tightly pressed that it seemed lipless. "Unpack that suitcase. I'm your husband. Don't ever forget that."

"Husband?" She did not intend for it to sound as scornful as it did, but she was reminded of the countless times when his futile love-making had left her sleepless for the rest of the night, of the following draggy, listless days when she could not forget or forgive him, when she had realized how completely she was being wasted. Memory drove the words out of her against her will, "You're not even the father of my baby."

She was sorry the minute the words left her mouth. She was frightened, too, for she saw Ronnie step back as if he had been jolted by a physical blow; she saw his face go bright red as it did occasionally when his anger fled beyond his control. He started toward her, cursing her, something he had never done before.

"You floozy," he said. "You God-damned floozy! You think I didn't know? You think I'm not reminded every time I look at your kid? I should have known the day I married you what you were."

He was within a step of her then and she screamed; his fingers fastened on her throat and he flung her on her bed, his thumbs pressed against her windpipe so she couldn't breathe. She struggled. She twisted and kicked and beat at him with her fists, but he was stronger than she had thought and she could not break free.

She was losing consciousness when Maggie Nolan, who had heard her scream, ran into the room. She grabbed Ronnie's arms and broke his grip on Janice, all the time yelling at the top of her voice, "Mr. Purvis, you don't know what you're doing."

He stepped back and wiped a sleeve across his face. He was panting as if he had just come in from a long run. He said hoarsely, "Don't ever tell anyone what you just saw. Do you understand that, Maggie?"

"I understand, Mr. Purvis," she said. "You were just beside yourself."

"Yes." He licked his lips, eyes turning to Janice who was still struggling for breath, then he turned and strode out of the room.

When she had her strength back so she could walk, Janice went to the livery stable and said to Pete Walker, "I want a horse and buggy immediately. I have to make a fast trip to Rawlins. I will leave the rig at the Red Front livery stable and you can have someone bring it back. I'll pay you for the use of the rig and for a man's wages to return them."

Pete shifted his weight from his crippled leg and scratched the back of his neck. "I'm right sorry, Mrs. Purvis. I can't let you have one."

"I can handle any horse that's broken," she said impatiently. "When we lived in Colorado I had a horse of my own, but when we moved Mr. Purvis sold it. I drove a great deal when we lived there. I won't have any trouble."

"It ain't that." Pete backed up a step. "I'm sorry, Mrs. Purvis. I just can't let you have a horse and rig. Your husband, he said not to. I'm in debt on this stable. I'm paying the bank big payments every month, and if I went agin what your husband said, well, I'd lose everything I've got. I tell you I'm sorry, but that's the way it is."

She left, knowing there was no use to argue, that Ronnie was God in Dead Horse as he wanted to be. She was a prisoner. There was no other place where she could turn for help. Even if she was allowed to take the stage, she would be too late getting to Rawlins. Al would look for her at the time she had said she would be there, and when she didn't come, he would leave. She couldn't blame him. He would never know what had happened.

She returned to the house and went to bed, sick with the frustration and helplessness she felt. Ronnie never mentioned what had happened. Apparently he took it for granted that she understood the situation and would never try it again.

Three days later Jerry was kidnapped.

CHAPTER XVIII

DREWS expected Whipple about half past ten. He wished he had told the man to come an hour earlier. It would take time to walk to the hotel, more time to find a vacant room from which they could watch Janice's door. And there was always the chance that Bentley would be so overcome by his anticipation and lust that he would not wait until midnight.

Drews paced around his living room, too nervous to sit down. He had smoked so much during the day that his mouth was hot and dry. He had burned his tongue, but still he kept a pipe going in his mouth. It gave him something to do with his hands; it was a sort of release from the nervous pressure that came from the waiting. He had to do something to take his mind off the minutes that were slowly piling up, one after another.

Whipple still had not come at fifteen minutes before eleven. It was early, but Drews thought Whipple would be early. Drews remembered how he had found him that afternoon, frightened almost into hysteria. He remembered how the editor had sat with his legs pressed together, and when he had stood up Drews had noticed the long, dark streak down the front of his pants. At the time he hadn't thought anything about it, but now he remembered and he realized what had happened.

Drews strode out through the front door, intending to go after Whipple. It was still ten minutes before the hour. He might miss Whipple in the darkness, then maybe miss him again as he returned to his own house. Drews went back in. He'd better wait. If he didn't need Whipple to call the Governor, he'd go to the hotel and quit worrying about him.

The trouble was Drews had called the Governor so many times asking for an investigation and a stay of execution, only to be turned down repeatedly, that he doubted the Governor would even talk to him this time, regardless of the evidence. But Whipple had been on the other side all along; he still held a seat in the legislature, and his *Bugle* was the only clear voice for the party in this section of the state. The Governor was quite aware of these facts. He would listen to Whipple.

Drews sat down, then he got up. He knocked his pipe out, filled it, and lighted it. He dropped a hand into his coat pocket, wanting to feel the comfortable grip of the gun butt, then realized he had left it with Janice.

He glanced at his watch again. Three minutes until eleven. He would wait those three minutes and no longer. He stepped into his bedroom, opened a drawer of his bureau and lifted a revolver from it. It was a newer gun than the one he had given Janice, with a longer barrel and therefore harder to carry, but he had no choice.

Taking it into the front room, he checked to see that the revolver was loaded. It was a double-action Colt with a six-inch barrel. He slipped it under his waistband, looked at his watch again, and saw that it was one minute after eleven. He went out through the door on the run, leaving the lamp burning on the center table in the front room.

Whipple did not live far from Drews's house. Even in the night blackness, and with few lights anywhere in town at this hour, Drews reached Whipple's place in less than three minutes. The house was dark. Whipple was probably in bed.

Drews pounded on the front door, his temper at the boiling point. He had known all the time he could not completely trust the editor, but he had not expected the man to fail him so completely. He pounded on the door again, and when he heard nothing, he tried to open it, but it was locked. He backed up and slammed the sole of his boot against the bottom of the door, but it was solid.

A lamp came to life inside. Whipple yelled, "All right, all right, I'm coming." A moment later he left his bedroom, set a lamp on the claw-footed table in the middle of his front room, then unlocked and opened the door. He was wearing a long, white nightgown; he looked at Drews, blinking owlishly as he ran a hand through his hair.

"Say, it isn't eleven, is it, Linc?" Whipple asked. "I wonder if I set my alarm clock wrong?"

Drews grabbed him by both arms. "By God, Alex, if I didn't need you tonight, I'd let you sleep, but I've got to have you. Get into some clothes."

"Now hold on," Whipple cried shrilly. "I didn't aim to oversleep. You've got no call to start roughing . . ."

"Get into some clothes," Drews shouted. "A promise doesn't mean a damned thing to you, does it? A man's life doesn't mean anything, either. Well, I'll tell you one thing. If something happens to Janice Purvis because you went to bed tonight instead of keeping your word, you'll wish you'd never been born."

Whipple scooted for his bedroom. Mrs. Whipple had lighted another lamp. She slipped into a worn robe and came into the front room, her face flushed with anger.

"You stop that kind of talk, Lincoln Drews," Mrs. Whipple said. "You just get out of here and let Alex alone. If he doesn't want to go with you and take part in this crazy, dangerous scheme you thought up, I guess he doesn't have too."

Drews walked toward her. He stopped a step away and stared at her white face. He said, "Does an innocent man's life mean anything to you, Madge? Or the safety of a woman who is risking her decency for that life? It does to me, and Alex is going to help like he promised."

"If you're talking about that killer Cobb," Mrs. Whipple flung at him, "you know he's not innocent. As for Janice Purvis, all I can say is that any woman who has men look at her the way she does is a . . . ."

White-faced, Drews said, "You'd better stop right there, Madge." She moved back from him, frightened. He said, "Madge, did you ever know of Alex doing a really good thing, a brave thing? Did you ever know him to believe in anything enough to stand up on his hind legs and fight for it?"

Whipple hurried out of the bedroom. "You don't need to answer that question, Madge. Linc knows the answer as well as you do." He yanked a closet door open and slapped a hat onto his head, his shame riding him hard. He pulled a coat off a hanger and put it on. "Come along, Linc."

They went out together. Drews looked at Mrs. Whipple, who stood with her back against the wall, hating him with all the fury of an aroused mother hen. Out in the street Drews started to run. He had worried about Janice until he was on the verge of giving way to panic. He had to know if she was all right.

If Bentley as much as laid a fat hand on Janice, Drews would beat him into a mass of jelly, and he would never forgive himself or Whipple for letting it happen.

CHAPTER XIX

JANICE had not intended to drop off to sleep when she lay down to wait for Bentley, but she did. The worry and strain from waiting had been too much. The tap on her door woke her, but for a moment she could not move; she felt as if she were in a very deep pool and no matter how hard she struggled, she could not break water.

The tap came again, louder this time. She rose, her mind still fuzzy, and, crossing to the door, opened it. The sight of Fred Bentley standing in the hall shocked her awake as quickly as a cold shower would have done.

He pushed past her into the room without waiting for an invitation. He said, "I was beginning to think you didn't mean what you said this afternoon and had pulled out."

Embarrassed, she put a hand to her hair and pushed some of the pins back into place. "I'm sorry, Fred. I went to sleep. I guess I'm not very pretty."

"You're always pretty to me," he said, attempting to be gallant.

She closed the door, worry nagging at her as she wondered if Lincoln Drews was in the hotel and had seen Bentley come in. Bentley stood in the middle of the room, his gaze undressing her as it moved down her body. She shivered, an involuntary reaction to the expression of naked lechery on his face. He moved toward her, but she side-stepped neatly, so that his outstretched hand barely brushed her negligee.

"Let's not be in a hurry, Fred," she said as she walked

toward the bureau. "We have all night, haven't we?"

She reached the bureau before he answered. She glanced at her watch as she picked up the bottle of whisky. It was fifteen minutes after eleven. Drews would not be here for three-quarters of an hour. She thought in despair that she could not stall Bentley that long.

As she turned toward him, he said roughly, "No, I ain't got all night. I don't like a woman who gives me the come-on the way you have and then plays hard to get."

She set the bottle back on the bureau. "All right, Fred." She motioned toward the door. "If you don't like me, I guess you'd better leave. You said you'd be here at midnight, you know. Well, I don't like men who show up almost an hour before they say they will."

"I said *about* midnight. I got away sooner than I expected to."

"Then you can leave earlier than you expected to. Maybe it'd do you some good if you went away and thought about it for an hour. Maybe you need to think about how much you like me."

He blinked, his forehead furrowed as he tried to figure out how she had forced him to take the defensive. He said, "Now hold on, Janice. You know I like you. It's got nothing to do with me being here early. I came when I could. I liked you the first time I saw you. You knew it, too. It's something a woman feels."

"Maybe I did. Maybe I didn't."

She stood by the bureau, the whisky bottle in her hand. She smiled, trying to hold her advantage and still hide the terrifying fear that sent the shivers down her spine. Until this moment, she had not realized how much she was depending on Lincoln Drews.

She asked herself how she was going to hold Bentley off until Drews came. She had no answer. She felt his eyes on her, staring as if he could not take his gaze from her, then he started toward her again.

Quickly she pulled the cork from the bottle and, picking up a glass, poured a stiff drink and held it out. She said, "They tell me this is very good whisky. I bought the best I could get for this occasion."

He took the proffered glass. "What the hell! You say maybe, but you buy a bottle of whisky and call this an occasion. That don't sound like maybe to me."

She motioned toward the glass of whisky. "Try it. Tell me whether it's good or not."

She had hoped that the whisky would loosen his tongue, but now she realized it might make him harder to handle. Only a few minutes had passed since he had come into the room. It was still more than half an hour before Drews would get here.

"I don't need the whisky," he said.

Once more he moved toward her, but she slipped away from him. "You're not very polite, Fred. I buy the whisky for you and I pour you a drink, but you just stand there holding it."

"All right, all right." He lifted the glass and took one swallow. He set the glass on the bureau, nodding. "It is good whisky. I didn't suppose you could buy anything like this in Dead Horse."

She sighed, shaking her head. "Fred, I don't know about you. You're such a direct man. You go right after the things you want. Maybe that works with some women, but I'm not some women."

"What do you mean?"

"I'm not your wife," she answered. "I'm not one of the women you buy in Rawlins, either." She shook her head again. "I expect a little talk, a little courting, and certainly the courtesy of seeing you drink the whisky I bought for you."

"I don't know about courting," he said glumly. "I'm a direct man just like you said, but I can drink the whisky if that'll do any good." He picked up the glass and finished the liquor that was in it. He set the empty glass down and wiped a sleeve across his mouth. "Now we'll start the courting. Come here."

"Just how do you start courting?"

"By kissing you, damn it. I said to come here."

She laughed as if amused as she saw how inept he was at this ageless game. "Your women haven't trained you very well, Fred. You've always talked as if you were a great hand with women. The talk comes first, you know. You just kind of lead into the courting."

He swore under his breath. "All right, what'll we talk about?"

"Oh, we might start with my husband. Or your wife. What would they think if they knew we were together in a hotel room?"

He grinned. "Your husband wouldn't like it, would he? He's the kind who figgers he don't have to share nothing he's got with anybody. As far as my wife goes, she don't care much one way or the other, as long as it don't get out. If I find another woman, I don't bother her none and that's the way she likes it. Now what do we talk about?"

She hesitated, wondering if she could afford to gamble on Drews coming early. She decided she had to. She might not be able to bring Bentley to this point again.

"Well, now that we've disposed of our mates," she said, "we might talk about Al Cobb. I knew him a long time ago. He wasn't as bad as Ronnie says he was."

"Cobb?" Bentley's lips curled as if the name were a dirty word. "I don't know what you ever saw in him. He's just another two-bit outlaw who thinks he's a hard case."

"He only has a little over 12 hours to live," she said. "It doesn't seem right. He kidnapped Jerry and brought him back, and that's what you arrested him for. But he was tried for the murder of Lee Fawcett, and that's what they're going to hang him for. There's no justice in that, Fred."

"Why not? He admits he killed Lee."

"Oh, I suppose he killed him, all right, but I don't think it was murder. He should be punished for stealing Jerry, but I've thought all along that he was telling the truth about running into Fawcett on the trail and Fawcett started to shoot at him. After all, three shells in Fawcett's gun had been fired. You don't hang a man for killing another man in self-defense."

"Cobb's going to hang." Bentley turned and, picking up the whisky glass, poured another drink. "You're purty smart at that, Janice. I figger it was self-defense, all right. Lee was jumpy about the deal from the beginning. When he seen Cobb coming down the trail with your boy in his arms, he was smart enough to know he was in a hell of a lot of trouble if somebody figgered out he was the one who took the kid. So he yanked his gun out and started shooting. Probably never figgered he might hit the boy. He never was one to figger anything out, Lee wasn't."

"You said Lee was jumpy. Then you must have known about it all the time."

"Sure I knew about it." He drank the whisky that was in the glass and put it down. "I don't know why you left Purvis 'cept that he just ain't man enough for you. Taking the boy was his idea all the time. I guess that was something you didn't know about your husband. He paid Lee $500 to take the kid and keep him in that cabin. He didn't aim for nothing to happen to the boy. He said you was talking about leaving him, and he was going to keep the kid out of your reach so you couldn't get him. He said he didn't give a damn whether you left or not, but he wasn't giving up the boy. I always figured he was pretending to love the kid so it would look good. He's such a cold fish, but I was wrong. He's crazy about the boy."

"Then you knew all the time where Jerry was?" she said accusingly.

"Yeah, sure I did, but like I said, Purvis just wanted him hid out where you couldn't find him. I knew he'd be all right. Lee was with him most of the time. He had to show up once in a while in town. Folks would have started wondering where he was, if he didn't. When he did leave, he locked the cabin. I ain't figgered how Cobb happened to find the boy. Just luck, I guess."

She turned and crossed the room to the door. This was all they needed to know. If Drews had heard . . . She opened the door, but he wasn't there. The hall was empty.

She heard Bentley come toward her, but she couldn't move. She wanted to scream that Bentley had just cleared Al Cobb, scream it so loud that the whole world would hear. But it wouldn't do any good. Everything Bentley had said was wasted. Now it was only her word against his.

She whirled to face him, knowing that her plan had failed because Bentley had come earlier than he had said he would. She had told herself that she would do anything to save Al, even to giving herself to Bentley. But now that the moment was here, she knew she could not do it, not even to save Al Cobb's life. She would kill Bentley first. He stopped and was staring at her.

"Get out of here." She motioned toward the open door. "Get out."

"No," he said. "You've had your fun with me. Now I aim to have mine."

She stood with her back pressed against the wall, so frozen by fear she could not move. The gun Drews had given her was under her pillow. It might just as well have been a mile away.

Then Bentley began to walk toward her, smiling in anticipation.

CHAPTER XX

DREWS was fifty feet ahead of Whipple when he reached the hotel. He stopped just inside the lobby door, looking around for Harvey Pearson but not seeing him. The lobby was usually deserted this time of night, for Pearson habitually spent the tag end of the evenings in the Stockman's Bar, along with the drummers and cowboys who were staying in town overnight.

Suddenly it struck Drews that this was the height of stupidity. He had been in a tremendous hurry to get here, but he hadn't thought out exactly what he would do. He was sure of just one thing. He couldn't stay here in the lobby. Bentley had said he would see Janice at midnight, so he probably intended to make his nightly round before he called on her. He'd be coming along Main Street any time now and Drews couldn't afford to be seen by him.

He wheeled, colliding with Whipple who was just coming through the door. Drews grabbed him by the arm, and hustled around the hotel into the blackness of the vacant lot next to the building.

"What the hell?" Whipple said. "I thought we were . . ."

"Yeah, we are," Drews said, "but we're not going to sit down in the lobby and take a chance on Bentley seeing us. Or going upstairs and running into him in the hall. We've got to figure this out right or we'll spoil the whole thing."

"We can go upstairs and hide in the room next to Mrs. Purvis's," Whipple suggested.

"And if some drunk cowboy happens to have that room," Drews said, "and comes in while we're listening to what Bentley's saying, we ruin Janice's scheme."

"You're worrying about shadows," Whipple said. "The alley will be as dark as the inside of a bull's gut. If we go up the back stairs he won't see us, unless we just happen to bump into him. Harvey only has one lamp burning in the hall and it's in the front. There'll be rooms on both sides of hers. It's not likely that both of them will be taken. We can see easily enough. You know which one she has, don't you?"

"It's 12. In the back right next to the alley stairs." Drews grabbed the editor's arm. "Hell, that's it. There's a big landing at the top of the stairs. If we get on the end of it, we'll be next to Janice's window and we can hear what's going on and we won't have to stand in the hall outside her door. Come on."

Drews led the way along the side of the hotel to the alley, stumbling over tin cans and bottles and other debris that had been thrown into the weeds. He reached the alley and stopped, one hand swinging out to hold Whipple behind him. The editor had been right about it being dark here. There was no light anywhere along the alley except from Janice's room above him, and she had pulled the green shades so that her windows were dark.

Drews waited a full minute. Hearing nothing except the faint clink of a tin can being rattled by some animal hunting for food, Drews whispered, "Take it slow and easy on the stairs. He might be up there ahead of us."

"Sure," Whipple muttered. "Slow and easy."

Drews felt his way along the rear of the building to the stairs. He paused again, thinking there was a chance Bentley might go by in the alley. It was his habit to make a midnight check of the alleys as well as the streets. Hearing nothing, Drews climbed the stairs to the landing, Whipple behind him. He moved quickly past the door that led into the hall and moved on toward

Janice's window. He heard Janice's voice, shrill and filled with fear, "I never intended to go through with this. All I wanted was for you to clear Al. Get out now and let me alone."

"You'll go through with it," Bentley said. "You got me to say what you wanted me to, and I'm guessing Drews or somebody was supposed to be out there in the hall listening. I got here early, so your scheme didn't work, but that didn't . . ."

Drews didn't wait to hear any more. He charged past Whipple, yanked back the door that opened into the hall, and plunged through it. So Bentley had said what Janice had wanted him to, but he had got here too late to hear it. He tried to turn the knob of Janice's door, but it was locked. He backed up and drove a shoulder against it. The door slammed open. One glance showed him that his worst fears were justified.

Bentley was holding Janice on the bed, but she was twisting and kicking, one tightly fisted hand beating at his face. Drews crossed the room in long strides, the hunger to kill blotting out every other emotion in him. Bentley, hearing the door crash open, swung around, but Drews was on him before he fully realized what was happening. His fists were half raised when Drews smashed him in the face with a driving right.

Bentley went back against the wall, his feet slipping out from under him. He sat down hard as Janice scrambled off the bed on the other side and stood with her back against the far wall, her right hand holding the negligee together where Bentley had torn it off one shoulder.

Bentley rolled over on his side and yanked his gun

from its holster. Drews kicked him savagely on the arm, sending the revolver flying through the air to bang against the wall. He caught Bentley by the shoulders and hauled him upright. He hit the sheriff on one side of the face and then the other, sledging blows that swiveled his head back and forth.

Bentley's knees buckled and he sprawled backward across the bed. He lay there, blood streaming down his battered face. Whipple stood in the doorway, repelled and yet drawn to this turbulent scene which had suddenly erupted in front of him.

A drummer, awakened by the noise, appeared in the doorway still pulling on his pants. Janice screamed at Whipple, "Shut the door."

Whipple shoved the man back into the hall. "It's a private fight," he said, and slammed the door in his face.

Bentley started to sit up on the bed. Drews slugged him in the face, knocking him flat again. He jumped on Bentley, knees digging into the man's soft belly, the desire to kill still a raging torment in him. He caught the sheriff by the throat, thumbs pressing against his windpipe.

"Lincoln." Janice shook Drews's shoulders. "Lincoln, you're killing him."

But she couldn't shake him loose; she couldn't break through his consciousness. She cried, "Whipple, help me. He's going to kill Bentley."

Whipple ran up on the other side of the bed. He grabbed one arm and Janice the other, but still they could not loosen his hold on Bentley's throat. The sheriff had almost stopped struggling, and his face was beginning to turn purple.

Janice gave up in despair. She looked around the room, saw the pitcher on the bureau, and, picking it up, threw the water into Drews's face. It shocked him. He looked at her, blinking.

"Stop it, Lincoln," she said. "We'll never get him to talk if you kill him."

Whipple was still trying to loosen Drews's hand on Bentley's throat. Now sanity showed in Drews's eyes. He sat back, his hands dropping to his sides. Janice had backed across the room again, once more closing her negligee with her hand.

Drews got off the bed and stood staring at Bentley, breathing hard as the murder lust began to die. Bentley's eyes were bulging like two oversized marbles, his big chest heaving as he labored for breath. Drews walked around the bed to Janice. He asked, "Did he . . . did he . . . ?"

She shook her head. "No, Lincoln," she whispered. "I'm . . . I'm all right."

"What did Bentley say?"

"He told me what we wanted to know. Ronnie paid Lee Fawcett $500 to kidnap Jerry and keep him in that cabin. Bentley knew where Jerry was all the time. Ronnie told them he wanted the boy hidden where I couldn't find him. He said I had threatened to leave him and he wasn't going to let me take Jerry."

Drews turned to Bentley who was sitting up, a hand feeling of his throat. Drews said, "You son of a bitch! So you knew where the boy was all the time, but you were damned sure you didn't look in the right place."

Bentley licked battered lips, then wiped a sleeve across his nose that was still dripping blood. He said, "She's a God-damned liar."

"After he told me about it," Janice said, "I went to the door and opened it. If you'd been in the hall, you'd have heard what he told me, but you weren't."

"Bentley got here early," Drews said.

Janice glanced at the silent Whipple, then at Drews. "Is my word any good against his?"

Drews shook his head. If he and Whipple had heard, the three of them could have testified in court. Now Bentley's statement meant nothing. He would say in court, just as he had said a moment before, that Janice lied. Drews turned away sick with disappointment.

"Get out of here, Bentley," Drews said. "I want to kill you more than I ever wanted to do anything in my life. If I have to keep looking at you, I will."

Bentley got up and started toward his gun. "Leave it alone," Drews said sharply. "Just get out of here."

Bentley swung around and walked toward the door, holding a hand over his belly and leaning forward as if every step hurt him. He opened the door, ignoring Whipple, and stood there clutching the casing, his head turned so he could look at Drews. He said, "I'll get a gun and I'll be back. I'll throw you in jail for attempted murder."

Drews walked toward him. "You do that, Fred. You do that."

Uncertainty began working in Bentley. He said, "You'll get ten years."

"No, I'll get the rope," Drews said. "If you think I

wouldn't be glad to kill you for what you tried to do tonight, you're crazy. You'd better go the other way the next time you see me coming."

Bentley fled, fear breaking his wall of dignity, and sending him scurrying along the hall as fast as his battered body would go. Drews closed the door. He asked, "What do you think, Alex? Is it worth calling the Governor?"

Whipple shook his head. "I'll try, but I don't think it'll do any good. It's her word against Bentley's. And another thing, Purvis carries more weight with the Governor than I do. They must have talked about him running for the legislature. Bentley could make quite a stink about her letting him into her room, too. It would sure fix her testimony. I don't think we'd get anywhere."

Drews nodded, for that was exactly what he was thinking. "All right, Alex, you might as well go back to bed. I'll see you if I think of anything."

Whipple nodded and slipped out of the room, glad to get out of it. Drews looked at his watch. It was almost midnight. Twelve hours! They had come close, but not close enough, and all because Whipple had gone to bed instead of keeping his word.

"Oh, Lincoln," Janice said. "I tried. I tried so hard. I don't know of anything else to do."

She sat on the bed and began to cry. He dropped down beside her and put an arm around her. She laid her head on his shoulder, glad for the security of his arm, glad for this moment of peace, but despair was with it, too. She shivered and buried her face in his shirt, for she knew she could not face tomorrow.

CHAPTER XXI

F OR the first time in hours Drews was not conscious of the passing minutes. This was an experience from which Janice would not recover quickly, so he sat there holding her, sensing that she needed his comfort and his strength.

Presently she stirred and drew away. She said, "I guess you don't think I have any decency to have even thought of doing this."

He shook his head. "I don't think any less of you because of what's happened."

"I'm afraid you will when you know all of it," she said. "Will you wait in the hall while I dress? But don't leave. Please. I've been alone much of my life, but I never felt this way before. I . . . I just don't think I could stand being alone for the rest of the night."

"I'll wait," he said.

He left the room and walked along the hall slowly, too restless to remain still. He filled his pipe and smoked it, his mind on Janice. He wasn't at all sure that she was in love with Al Cobb, enough in love to take the risk she had taken tonight. He could think of only one other explanation, that she had somehow been caught in a trap from which there was no escape except self-abasement.

She opened the door and motioned for him to come in. She closed the door behind him and said, "Sit down, Lincoln. I want to talk. I didn't before. I guess I couldn't. I thought Al would tell you. Or maybe you'd find out some other way, but of course you couldn't. Ronnie wouldn't tell, and if he did, most of what he said would be lies."

"You don't have to tell me anything, if it's too difficult," he said.

"Of course it's difficult. Wouldn't it be difficult for you to tell someone else about an act of complete selfishness, on your part, which had ruined a man's life? I did that to Al. He had a hard life as a boy, so what I did simply made certain what he would be and do."

"Don't tell me," he said. "I'll take any woman on faith who shows the courage . . ."

"No, Lincoln," she interrupted. "It was cowardice. It was the only way I could free myself. Now I want to tell you. Maybe I'll feel better. I guess that's why so many people confess their sins to their priests. It kind of purifies them just to tell someone what they've done wrong."

He nodded, understanding that, and sat down on the foot of the bed and filled his pipe. She walked around the room, frowning, her hands clenched at her sides, then she sat down at the head of the bed, her bare feet tucked under her, and began to talk.

She started with her sophomore year in high school, telling her story as objectively as she could, leaving out nothing except what had happened in Fortune the morning Al Cobb had come to her when she was currying the bay gelding in the barn.

"When I didn't show up in Rawlins at the time I had written I would," she said, "Al came here to Dead Horse. He'd guessed I'd run into trouble. At least, he said, he wanted to hear me say with my mouth that I didn't want to go with him. It was dark when he came to the house.

165

That was just a little while after Jerry was kidnapped, and I was alone. Ronnie had gone downtown to see if the search parties had found anything."

She stopped and stared at her folded hands that rested on her lap. "I guess we'll never know exactly what happened when Jerry was taken, but Ronnie must have had Fawcett waiting in the alley. I was late getting home that night and Ronnie had let Lena leave. Maggie Nolan was gone, too. Ronnie was alone with Jerry. He must have spent a long time planning it out. Maybe he was playing with Jerry in the back yard. Or maybe he left Jerry alone, and Jerry wandered out behind the barn into the alley and Fawcett got him. It's all mixed up in Jerry's mind and I've been afraid to press him about it.

"Anyhow, when I got home, Ronnie was all worked up about Jerry having run away. When we found out he had been kidnapped, Ronnie took on about it in public so everybody would think he was the grief-stricken father. Nobody but me and Lena knew how he really felt. That's part of him, you see. He can't stand to lose money, and he can't stand public disgrace of any kind. That's why he kept going downtown to ask about the search parties, and acting as if he just couldn't stand it if Jerry wasn't found."

She paused, glancing briefly at Drews, then went on, "When Al came, I told him what had happened. I felt sure Ronnie was responsible for the kidnapping. He had hinted at it by saying he guessed I wouldn't leave him as long as Jerry was lost. I believe that if I had promised I'd never try to leave him again, he would have had Fawcett bring Jerry in, but I didn't think of it then. I wasn't able to think of anything, really. I just wanted Jerry back, so when Al came, I asked him to hunt for Jerry.

"I was sure that if Ronnie had taken Jerry, he wouldn't have hidden him very far from town. Ronnie would have to take food to him and still be here most of the time. Besides, Ronnie hates horses. It seemed to me he'd find a hiding place within walking distance of town, but not right in town because someone would hear Jerry crying.

"The next morning Al started riding a circle around town. He gradually widened it so sooner or later he was bound to stumble onto the right cabin. I didn't have any idea Fawcett was the one who had taken Jerry. The lucky part was that Al found Jerry when Fawcett was gone. I don't know what would have happened if Fawcett had been there. If Al had just ridden off that night after he'd talked to me instead of looking for Jerry, he'd be safe now, so you see I'm to blame even for this trouble he's in."

"We still have a little time," Drews said.

"You've thought of something?" she asked hopefully.

He shook his head, giving her a crooked grin. "I was just trying to be optimistic. Right now it looks to me as if Purvis is the only one who can save Al."

"Why, Ronnie wouldn't lift a finger to save Al," she cried. "He hates him more than he loves his own life."

Drews nodded, thinking that he had misjudged Purvis more than he had ever misjudged a man in his life. He looked at Janice, sensing the misery that was in her, that would go on torturing her all of her life if Al Cobb hanged at high noon tomorrow.

He said gently, "You've blamed yourself for years

because you think you're responsible for Al turning out the way he has, but you're wrong. He's that kind of man, Janice. He's not the bad man Whipple has made him in the newspaper, but he's a loner and he's tough. He wouldn't want the responsibility of a wife and children, and even if he hadn't gone to the reform school, something else would have happened that would have set him against society."

"I wish I could believe that," she said.

She slid off the bed and walked around the room again, too restless to sit still. "You were right when you asked me after dinner today if I could have lived Al's kind of life. I didn't answer you. I couldn't. You see, that's something I have never been honest about even with myself, but I know it would have been a terrible mistake to have gone away with him. I'd have left him within a year because I couldn't raise Jerry that way."

She came to the bed and sat down beside Drews. "I want your respect more than the respect of any man I ever met. That's why I didn't tell you one thing that's important. Ronnie isn't Jerry's father. Al is. It happened the time he was in Fortune." She stared at the wall on the other side of the room. "I'm not ashamed of it, Lincoln. I wanted a baby and Ronnie couldn't give it to me."

She turned her head and looked at him defiantly. "Now you know why Ronnie hates Al as much as he does. He could never forgive another man for doing something he was not capable of doing. And I guess it's why I . . . I knew I had to try to save Al, so I went to you. I couldn't let Jerry's father hang, no matter what price I had to pay to save him."

So that was it, Drews thought. He should have guessed. Now that he thought about Jerry's round face, and strong little body and curly blond hair, he told himself that the child did look like Al and not at all like Ronald Purvis. It explained Purvis's hatred, too. Knowing the banker as he did now, he understood how the man's burden of failure as a husband would fill him with the insane hatred that he had for Al Cobb.

"That explains a lot of things," Drews said. "If Al hadn't found the boy when he did, Purvis might have killed him."

She nodded. "He would do it to hurt me." She hesitated, her gaze touching his face and turning away again. She said, "It must seem strange to you that I would stay with Ronnie as long as I have. I guess I was just a coward. I couldn't face earning a living for myself. I didn't have any training. I would have had to take in washing or be a waitress or something like that, so it was easier to swallow my pride and get along with Ronnie than to strike out for myself. And I was afraid, too. I knew how vindictive he was, and that he'd find some way to hurt me and Jerry. He's so warped and twisted that he can't think of anything except injuring me and Al and building himself up."

Drews looked at her, understanding how much it hurt her to admit she had been a coward. This same cowardice, he thought, was responsible for her failure to speak up during the trial and the days that followed. She had been afraid for herself and Ronnie, and perhaps equally afraid of the public disgrace that would be hers once she confessed in court that Al Cobb was the father of her child.

He looked at his watch. It was a few minutes after two. A little less than 10 hours. He said, "I'm going to see Purvis. I don't suppose it will do any good, but I'm going to try. And I'll see Bentley again. Maybe if I scare him enough . . ."

A knock on the door interrupted him. He rose and, glancing at Janice, saw that she wasn't going to get up. He wasn't sure she was able to. He crossed the room and opened the door. Lena Walker stood in the hall. She was trembling, her face so white that Drews thought she was ill. She glanced at him, then she saw Janice and stepped into the room.

Lena said, her tone little more than a whisper, "Your husband has Jerry, Mrs. Purvis. I just couldn't help it. I didn't even know about it until it had happened, and then it was too late to keep him from taking Jerry."

CHAPTER XXII

JANICE put her feet on the floor and started to get up, but her strength had drained out of her until she could not bring herself upright. She stared at Lena, her hands palm-down on her lap, her face turning so white that Drews thought she was going to faint. She opened her mouth to say something, but no words came out.

She sat there, staring at Lena, but she probably didn't see the girl at all. Watching her, Drews knew how she felt. She had tried to provide for the safety of her child, but still the tragedy she had been most afraid of had actually happened. If the boy was killed, she would never know a minute's peace or happiness. It would be far worse on her than if Al Cobb was hanged at high noon tomorrow.

"What happened, Lena?" Drews asked.

"I put Jerry to bed in a small room beside mine," Lena answered. "He went to sleep right away. I stayed up a while until I saw that he was going to sleep all right, then I went to bed. Pa gets home late from the livery stable, usually after midnight. Sometimes it's later, if he stops at the Stockman's Bar for a drink. I never stay up for him, so I didn't think about doing it tonight. I left my door open so I'd be sure to hear Jerry if he woke up during the night."

She glanced at Janice and brought her eyes back to Drews. "Well, Mr. Purvis was waiting outside for Pa when he came home. He said there had been a mistake, that he and Mrs. Purvis had intended to be gone all night, but their plans had changed. They were home, and he'd come to get Jerry. Pa lighted a lamp and showed him where Jerry was. Mr. Purvis said to be real quiet and Jerry wouldn't wake up. I guess he didn't because I didn't hear anything.

"I don't know what woke me up. Maybe I had a dream. Anyhow, I was scared. I was sitting up in bed. Right away I thought about Jerry and I went into the other bedroom to see if he was all right, but he was gone. I ran into Pa's room. He told me what had happened. Of course he thought he done right. I didn't tell him what you said, Mrs. Purvis. I guess I should have, but I don't think it would have made any difference. He's so scared of Mr. Purvis he would have given Jerry to him anyway."

She was looking at Janice now, wanting to be forgiven, but Janice did not say anything. She was staring at the girl and still not seeing her, Drews thought. Perhaps she hadn't even heard all that the girl said.

"It isn't your fault, Lena," Drews said. "You run along now. Jerry is probably home in his own bed."

Lena started toward the door, then stopped and looked back at Janice as if not sure what she should do. "It's all right, Lena." Drews caught her arm and led her out of the room and into the hall. "You go on home. Mrs. Purvis isn't well, so I'll go to her house and have a look, but I'm sure Jerry will be all right with his father."

"You don't know how it is, Mr. Drews," the girl said. "Nobody knows what Mr. Purvis is unless you've been there in his home a long time, like me and Maggie. He's a cruel man, Mr. Drews. I don't know what he might do."

She began to cry. Drews patted her shoulder. "I know all about him, Lena. I'll go up there right away and see about it. Now you get for home. Don't you or your Pa go up there. Purvis is alone and he might get nervous and shoot you."

She looked at him a moment, then wiped her eyes and, turning, walked away. Drews went back into the room. He said, "I'll go to your house and get Jerry. You think he's there?"

"Yes," she said. "He's there. Ronnie's afraid of the dark. He won't take Jerry away until it's daylight. I don't think he'll take him away even then. This is his way of making me swallow my pride and come back to him. If I do, he'll feel he's won and isn't publicly disgraced. If I don't, he'll kill my baby."

She swallowed with an effort. "I'd better go, Lincoln. It would make him worse if you go. He's unpredictable. He might even insist that Al has to be hanged before he lets me have Jerry. We can't be sure of anything, except that he'll make me crawl to him. I'll do it, if that's what it takes to save Jerry."

"I'm going with you," Drews said. "I can't let you go back alone. He'll kill you, too. Maybe he'll kill himself. He isn't sane, Janice."

"No, he'd never kill himself," Janice said. "I don't think he'd kill me. Just Jerry because that's the way he can hurt me the most."

Drews shook his head, doubting that Janice was right. Ronald Purvis had reached the place where he had stopped thinking as a human being.

Unless Janice went back to him, perhaps apologized publicly, he would destroy himself and her and the boy, rather than face the gossipy community. That was the way Drews thought it would be with this man who had never known how to live, and therefore had no inner resources to call to his help, now that he faced what to him was total disaster.

"We'd both better go," Drews said. "I'll let you talk to him. Maybe we won't have to let him know I'm there, but I'll be there just the same. You've got to live, Janice. It would be a poor thing for you to die and Jerry to live without a mother."

She rose, nodding. "All right, we'll both go, but you'll

have to let me talk to him alone. It would just set him off if he knew someone else was there."

He didn't argue. This was something that had to be played by ear, and neither he nor Janice would know what to do until they were there. As he left the room with her and walked down the hall toward the head of the stairs, he glanced at her face. She was still pale and extremely nervous, but he thought she was thinking coherently at least, and had recovered from the first deadening impact of shock that Lena's news had given her.

When they reached the lobby, they both stopped. Fred Bentley was standing by the desk, sullen eyes fixed on them, his face showing the battering that Drews's fists had given him.

"No trouble, Drews," Bentley said.

Drews stepped away from Janice, right hand dropping to the butt of his gun. He was in no mood to argue or even talk to Bentley, but if it came to a killing, he would not back away from it. His first thought was that Purvis had sent Bentley here to make sure that Janice came to the house alone.

"What do you want?" Drews asked.

"I still don't have a gun," Bentley said. "I ain't here to do you any favors, Drews, but I'm trying to do Mrs. Purvis one. Keep your hand away from your iron."

Drews did not loosen his grip on the butt of his gun. "I told you a while ago I'd rather kill you than not. If this is some kind of a trick Purvis thought up . . ."

"Hell, no," Bentley burst out. "I'm no damned good the way you figger, but by God, even a smart bastard like you can be wrong. I don't want no part of kid killing. That damned Purvis has gone clean loco. I thought all the time he liked the boy."

"What is it?" Janice cried. "Have you been to the house?"

Bentley nodded. "I just came from there. I wanted to talk to Purvis. I aimed to tell him you was in the hotel with Drews and when I tried to get you to go home, Drews beat hell out of me. I figgered he'd come back with me, but I never got to tell him nothing. Right off, soon as he saw me he said you'd better get back home right away, or you'd never see your boy alive again. Told me to tell you. Wouldn't listen to me at all."

Bentley licked his swollen lips. "When I got here, I didn't know what to do. I was afraid Drews would kill me if I went up there to your room, so I waited, figgering somebody would come in and I could send word to you, Mrs. Purvis, and Drews wouldn't know."

"How long, have you been here?" Drews demanded.

"Not very long."

"Did you see Lena Walker go out?"

Bentley shook his head. "I ain't seen nobody, or I would have got a message to Mrs. Purvis. You'd better hurry. I tell you he sounded loco and that's a fact. He said for you to come alone."

"All right, Bentley," Drews said.

He took Janice's arm and guided her across the lobby to the street door, his right hand still on the butt of his gun. He turned his head so he could watch Bentley until they were in the street. Then Janice jerked free from his grasp and began to run.

CHAPTER XXIII

THE night was pit black, with no lights showing anywhere in town, except in the hotel and the Stockman's Bar. Once Janice and Drews were off Main Street, the darkness was so complete that they found it difficult to even know exactly where they were. Janice, running ahead of Drews, tripped over a chunk and fell headlong into the street dust.

Drews helped her to her feet. He said gently, "Let's slow down. They say haste makes waste. In a case like this I guess it does."

He put an arm around her and held her so that her face was against his chest. She stayed that way for a time, breathing hard. He felt her tremble. She was nearly hysterical, he thought, and wondered if she could see this through to the end without going to pieces.

Presently she stopped trembling. She said, "You're right, Lincoln. Ronnie will wait until I get there before doing what he plans to do."

They climbed the slope, then paused for a moment outside the iron fence. Drews studied the sprawling house, its outline barely visible against the dark sky. The only light anywhere in the place was in the parlor.

Drews asked, "There's a carpet on the hall floor, isn't there?"

"Yes."

"I'll go in with you," he said in a low tone. "I won't say anything, so if you don't let on I'm there, he won't know you're not alone. You've got to find out where the boy is and get him out of the house, then I'll settle with Purvis."

"All right," she said. "He never likes to hear Jerry fuss, so he's probably put him to bed in his room."

"Probably," Drews said.

He agreed with Janice rather than worry her, but he thought she was wrong. Perverted by hate as Purvis was, and knowing that Al Cobb was Jerry's father, the chances were good, Drews thought, that the child was dead.

Janice opened the gate. The hinges squealed, the sound inordinately loud in the early morning quiet, loud enough so that Purvis very likely heard and therefore knew that Janice had come. They crossed the yard, then climbed the steps to the porch. Drews followed Janice to the door, moving slowly and carefully, afraid that the boards would squeak under his greater weight, and relieved when they didn't.

Janice opened the door and, stepping into the hall, called, "Ronnie."

"In here," he said. "In the parlor."

"Where's Jerry?" Janice asked.

"It took him to bring you back, didn't it?" Purvis said smugly. "I thought it would. Well, he's asleep. You're never leaving my house again, Janice. Do you under-stand that?"

"Yes, Ronnie," she answered, "but before we talk about that, I want to see Jerry."

"Why?" he demanded suspiciously. "You think I'm lying?"

"No Ronnie," she said. "I just want to see him. You

know how I am. I often get up in the night to see if he's kicked his covers off."

"He's all right," Purvis said. "I just looked at him. You come in here. Now."

She hesitated. Drews, standing next to the portieres that hung between the hall and the parlor, could not guess why Purvis was making this demand unless the boy wasn't in his bed at all. If Purvis had killed him, he might have the child's body in the parlor. He would want Janice to see it, then perhaps he would kill her. Instinctively Drews put a hand out and gripped Janice's shoulder, holding her there.

"By God, you'd better get in here," Purvis shouted. "You should have learned before now that my wife obeys me."

"Yes, Ronnie," she said. "Of course I've learned that. I just wanted to go upstairs to see Jerry."

"Get in here, damn it," he raged.

Drews knew this was the time for a showdown, and he believed he had thought of a way to break Purvis. In any case, he could not allow Janice to face her husband alone, as unpredictable as he was. He whispered, "I've changed my mind. You're not going to talk to him. I am."

He followed Janice into the parlor. Purvis stood beside the table in the middle of the room, so tall and thin he seemed grotesque. His face was flushed, and Drews, staring at him, wondered if he was about to have a stroke.

Purvis opened his mouth to say something when he saw Janice, then his gaze swung to Drews and he burst into a rash of oaths. He flung out an arm toward Drews. "Get out of here," he said thickly. "I told Bentley to tell her to come alone. Now get out."

"She's always obeyed you." Drews was relieved to see that Jerry was not in the room, so perhaps he really was asleep upstairs in his own bed. "I'm her lawyer, Purvis. I advised her not to come alone. That's why she didn't obey you this time. She should have had legal advice a long time ago."

"I'm her lawyer," Purvis shouted. "I'll give her all the legal advice she needs. I won't even talk to her while you're in the house. I'll take her back. I'll overlook all that she's done, but on my terms. Now get out of here or I won't even discuss them with her."

Drews stepped away from Janice. If it came to a shooting, he didn't want to be standing so close to her that she would be in danger. Purvis was trembling, his face darker than ever. He was, Drews thought, rapidly approaching the explosive point where he would lose his self-control, as he had when he had drawn his gun on Whipple in the bank.

"I'm not leaving," Drews said. "You'll discuss this settlement with me. I won't leave until you've signed an agreement which spells out the terms of the settlement, then we'll both leave and we'll take the boy with us."

"What kind of a settlement are you talking about?" Purvis demanded. "She's my wife. She's going to live in this house and act the way a mother ought to act, and she doesn't need a slick-tongued shyster spelling out any agreement."

"She's going to file for a divorce," Drews said, "and

she certainly doesn't intend to walk out with nothing. You're a rich man, Purvis. I'd say half of what you have would be about right."

Purvis tried to laugh, as if anything of the kind was ridiculous. "I thought you had more sense than that, Drews. She left me. I didn't leave her. You have no grounds to sue me for divorce. I said I'd take her back."

"She doesn't want to come back, and I assure you we have ample grounds for asking for a divorce. She's told me everything, and we'll bring it all out in court, if we have to. It's a lot of dirty linen to wash in public, but if it comes to that, we'll wash it. Everything, Purvis. I know why you hate Al Cobb. She's told me all about it. What's more, I know you tried to kill her and we can prove it in court. If Maggie Nolan won't testify to what you did, Lena Walker will."

"She didn't see it," Purvis screamed.

"So you admit it to me," Drews said with satisfaction. "You might be wrong about Lena. How do you know she wasn't in the hall and saw all that happened?" Drews shook his head. "I'll lay it out for you, Purvis. Either you sign the agreement I will draw up, or we'll go to court and you'll have facts come out that will ruin you and make you the laughing stock of Dead Horse. You won't be able to walk down the street without having people snicker at you. You don't want that to happen, Purvis."

"Judge Charnley is a friend of mine," Purvis said, his voice under control now. "You'll get nowhere in his court."

"I'll take you to the Supreme Court," Drews said. "It isn't just Dead Horse that will know about you. So will

Cheyenne. The Governor will hear the whole rotten story. I'll drag you through muck from here to Washington, Purvis. This is something you can't stand. You'll end up shooting yourself."

"I think not," Purvis said. "There are only three people who are dangerous to me. Al Cobb will be dead in a few hours. After tonight Janice can talk all she wants to, but nobody will believe her. Everyone knows she's a spiteful woman who deserted her husband and her child. I'm looking out for the boy. I'm willing to go on looking out for her, but she walked out on me. You think she'll cut any ice with anyone from now on? Why do you think I got the kid and brought him back into this house?"

"I guess the reason's plain enough," Drews said, "but you're overlooking the third person. I know, too, Purvis, and people will believe me."

"Yes, I must not overlook you," Purvis said, and drew his gun.

Drews had expected this, but not just at that exact moment. He yanked his gun out from under his waistband, surprised that Purvis had not exploded into a towering fit of rage as he had with Whipple, and because Drews had been surprised, he was a second slower getting his pistol into action than Purvis. The banker had one chance and he missed, the bullet slapping past Drews's head to slice through the portieres behind him and bury itself in the hall wall.

Drews fired before Purvis could level his revolver again. He caught the banker in the chest, the bullet driving Purvis back. Purvis's finger jerked the trigger again, a reflex action that sent the bullet slamming into the wall high above Drews's head. He folded, the gun slipping from slack fingers, and fell full length onto the thick carpet.

For a moment the sound of shots hammered against the walls and rolled back in continuing echoes of sound, as the cloud of powder smoke drifted upward toward the ceiling. Then the welcome sound of Jerry's crying came to Janice's ears. She cried out, "Jerry! He's all right." She whirled and ran into the hall and up the stairs, stumbling and falling in the darkness, and climbing again.

Drews, still holding his gun, walked to Purvis's body and, stooping, felt his pulse. The banker was dead. Drews straightened and slipped the revolver under his waistband again. Strange, he thought, that he, a man trained to use the courts and the law, was forced to settle this case with a gun.

He took the lamp from the table and went upstairs. Janice was on her knees beside Jerry's bed. She had the boy in her arms and was rocking him, soothing him with words of assurance. Drews set the lamp on the bureau, then knelt beside her and said softly, "Stay up here. I'll get Doc Chute to help me."

He rose and went down the stairs, walking slowly, one hand on the bannister. When he was outside, he looked back at the house, wondering what Janice would do. She could not continue to live here, he thought, so the house would stand as an empty monument to the memory of Ronald Purvis.

CHAPTER XXIV

B Y nine o'clock people began to arrive in Dead Horse for the hanging. Some who lived near the fringe of town came on foot. Others came on horses, or in buggies, hacks or wagons. One enterprising boy had popped a basket of corn and was selling it at a nickel a sack. Someone else had set up a lunch counter on a vacant lot across the street from the courthouse.

Lincoln Drews, standing in the doorway of the sheriff's office, watched and cursed under his breath. Men, women and children, whole families from grandpas on down to toddlers, had come to see Al Cobb lose his life, to swing at the end of a rope, his head twisted at a horrible, grotesque angle, his face turning purple, his eyes bulging from his head. A Roman holiday, Drews told himself bitterly. A free circus.

He turned to the desk where Bentley sat staring at him. The sheriff's eyes, swollen nearly shut, glittered with a vindictive hatred that he made no attempt to conceal. Drews had come early this morning and, having learned from Cobb that Bentley had eaten his supper the night before, and that Cobb had had nothing to eat for 24 hours, had brought him a substantial breakfast from the hotel dining room.

Drews had not promised Cobb that he would escape hanging. All he could say was that he was still working on it, then he returned to the office and sat down to wait for Bentley. He had decided against calling the Governor himself, or having Alexander Whipple do it. Fred Bentley had the best chance of securing a stay of execution, and he thought he knew how to get Bentley to make the call.

Drews pulled up a chair and sat down, his gaze on the sheriff's battered face. Bentley had arrived only a few minutes ago, moving slowly along Main Street as if it hurt him to walk. Drews had resolved to wait for him. If he had not put in his appearance by nine, Drews would have started looking for him. Drews had learned from experience that the Governor was irascible if called at his home at an early hour.

There was time enough between nine and noon to call the Governor, unless he was out of the capital or the wires were down. Drews had not decided what he'd do in either of those emergencies.

After Doc Chute had removed Purvis's body, Drews had promised Janice he would stop the hanging; but he had no idea how it could be accomplished unless the Governor stepped in. More than that, it would be suicide to use illegal force to take the crowd's anticipated entertainment away from it. In any case, that was a problem he hoped he wouldn't have to meet.

"You were late getting here this morning, Fred," Drews said.

"I went to bed for a while," Bentley said sullenly. "You gave me a hell of a beating. I ain't gonna forget it."

"No, you'd better remember it so you won't get another one," Drews said. "Now I'm going to tell you what to do. You're going to resign after a few days and sell your house and leave town with your wife, but it would discommode us if you did it today. You've got a couple of jobs to do this morning. You'll break up that crowd. Tell the people there won't be a hanging today. But before you do that, you're going to get on your phone and call the Governor and get a stay of execution for Al Cobb."

Bentley was so shocked by surprise that he seemed stunned, the hostility dying in him. He said, "My hearing has gone to hell. I guess you couldn't have said what I thought you said."

"You heard, all right," Drews said sharply. "We've got less than three hours to do it. Get busy."

"Well, by God," Bentley said. "I've called you a lot of names, none of 'em good, but I never called you a complete idiot before. Looks like that's what you are, though."

"No, I'm not an idiot," Drews said. "I can call the Governor. Whipple can, too. But you're a man the Governor will listen to, and I'm not sure he'll listen to me or Whipple. You know as well as I do that Cobb is innocent, so tell the Governor. If we get another trial, I'll get him off. You know that, too."

"Yeah, I know it, all right," Bentley said, "but I've got to go ahead and hang the bastard. There's no way I can tell the Governor what I know without putting my own neck in a noose, and I ain't aiming to do that. Why hell, I'd be admitting I was guilty of mal . . . mal . . ."

"The word is malfeasance," Drews said. "You would indeed, Fred. As a matter of fact, you were guilty of it. You knew what was happening all the time, and it's my guess you were paid to keep your mouth shut and look for Jerry where he wasn't. But I can't prove it, so I won't try. There are some other things I can prove, though.

Now I'm offering you a deal. If you don't take it, I'll clean your plow for you and don't you doubt it."

"If you lay a hand on me again . . ."

"No, I'm not going to right now, although I'd like to, but I'll tell you what I will do." Drews leaned forward, his gaze on Bentley's face, his grim expression that of a man who intended to do exactly what he said he would and wanted Bentley to know it. "I'll press charges against you for rape. Now you'd better think that over, Fred. First I'll go to your wife. I'll tell her what happened and that Whipple will put it in the *Bugle*. Second, Mrs. Purvis will testify in court that you raped her. She won't want to because it would mean a lot of dirty gossip, but she'll do it. Third, you'll be tried before Judge Charnley. You'd do well to remember a couple of things about him. He's very fond of Mrs. Purvis, and if there is a crime in the books that he hates, it's rape. You ought to know that from what's happened in his court on more than one occasion. He'll give you twenty years."

Bentley flinched, then tried to bluster. He said loudly, "Why hell, you can't make a charge like that stick. I didn't rape her. Besides, I was in her room at her invitation."

"We'll make it stick, all right," Drews said. "Going into a woman's room at her invitation does not give a man the right to do what you were doing, when Whipple and I showed up. As far as what you actually did is concerned, Mrs. Purvis will swear you did it, and Whipple and I will swear you had her on the bed and she was fighting as hard as she could. She certainly wasn't in that position by her own consent."

Still Bentley hesitated, trying desperately to find a way

out. Drews said slowly, "I don't have time to waste, Fred. Just remember that Ronald Purvis isn't alive to bail you out. You get over to that phone and do it now, or I'll see your wife this morning. If I know her, she won't perjure herself by swearing you were in bed with her when Whipple and I caught you in Mrs. Purvis's hotel room."

Bentley caved then, and it seemed ironical to Drews that the man was more afraid of his wife than he was of being sentenced to prison by Judge Charnley.

"All right," Bentley said sullenly. "How'm I'm going to tell him what I know without getting my tail in a crack?"

"You saw Purvis just before Janice and I went to the house," Drews said. "He told you what happened. He hated the boy. He planned to kill him. He'd had him kidnapped before and had paid Fawcett to do it. Don't you remember?"

"Yeah, I remember," Bentley said. "Get out of here while I talk to him. Shut the door, too. I don't want nobody listening."

Drews closed the street door and, picking up the ring of keys from the desk, walked toward the corridor. He stopped and said, "This isn't just a question of your trying, Fred. This is a proposition of succeeding. You can tell the Governor that Mrs. Purvis is prepared to testify in court that Cobb talked to her the night before, that she asked him to hunt for the boy and he promised he would. He brought the child to her the next day. No ransom was paid. If he didn't kidnap the boy, and we both know he didn't, Fawcett had no reason to arrest him, so Fawcett must have started shooting just as Cobb said he did.

Therefore the killing was self-defense."

"You didn't bring all that out in the trial," Bentley said.

"I didn't know it then. Cobb didn't tell it because he was trying to protect Mrs. Purvis's reputation. She didn't want it known that he had come to see her the night before while Purvis was gone, and she hadn't found the courage at that time to testify in court. She has now."

"All right," Bentley said and, getting up from his chair behind his desk, walked to the wall phone on the other side of the room.

Drews stepped into the corridor and, moving along it to Cobb's cell, unlocked the door and let himself in. Cobb was staring through the window at the gallows and the crowd that was milling around it. He glanced at Drews and tried to grin. "They're getting a little impatient," he said.

"They'll get more impatient," Drews said. "Bentley's phoning the Governor right now to get a stay of execution."

"Bentley!" Cobb sat down on his bunk. "Now that is the damnedest thing I ever heard. That fat bastard has wanted to put a rope on my neck so bad he could taste it."

Drews laughed shortly. "It's kind of funny, for a fact. Well, I changed his attitude toward the hanging. If he fails, he'll be the sorriest man in Dead Horse county."

"You must be blackmailing him," Cobb said.

Drews shrugged. "That's not a good word, Al. The truth is I never liked him much and last night I gave him a hell of a whipping. When you see his face, you'll know what I'm talking about."

"You're some lawyer," Cobb said admiringly. "A

lawyer beating up the sheriff. I wish I could have seen it."

"It wasn't much of a fight," Drews said. "He never hit me a lick." He handed Cobb a cigar and, taking a pipe and tobacco can out of his pocket, filled and lighted the pipe. He had told Cobb what had happened in the Purvis house, but he had not told him what had happened in Janice's hotel room. He was afraid that if he did, Cobb would kill Bentley if he was ever released from custody.

"I still would have liked to have seen it," Cobb said. "I wish I could have done it myself." He held the cigar in his hand, staring at it as he rolled it between his fingers. "Funny thing about Ronnie. He must have known Jerry was my son, not his. If he did know, you'd have thought he would have gone ahead and killed the boy."

Drews was so startled that he found it hard to keep his composure. He had not known that Janice had told Cobb that Jerry was his son, but obviously she had. He wondered if Cobb would feel any obligation, now that he knew the child was his. This had worried Drews from the first. It would be the final touch of tragedy, in his opinion, for Cobb to be acquitted and take Janice with him when he left Dead Horse.

"I didn't know Janice had told you," Drews said.

Cobb nodded, grinning a little. "Yeah, she told me the night I rode in from Rawlins and she said Jerry had been kidnapped. I wouldn't have gone looking for the boy if she hadn't. I wouldn't have ridden ten feet out of my way to find Ronnie's kid. I figured maybe she was lying, but I took a chance. When I got a look at him, I knew damned well he was mine."

Drews smiled, thinking that this man Cobb was filled

with many surprises. Then a new thought occurred to him, and he asked, "Did your knowing that have anything to do with your keeping still about you and Janice during the trial?"

The grin left Cobb's face. "Of course," he said gravely. "I knew I wasn't really worth a damn, and it didn't make a hell of a lot of difference whether they strung me up or not. As far as Janice was concerned . . ." He stopped, then he shrugged and went on, "No matter how much I think of her, the fact is she's been nothing but bad luck for me from the time we were in high school. But if all this had come out in the trial, everybody would have knowed it, and the kid would have been behind the eight ball from the start. This way he's respectable." The grin returned to Cobb's lips. "Maybe I'll never have another son. Who knows? Anyhow, I wanted to give the one I did have the best start I could."

The metal door opened and Bentley walked slowly toward Cobb's cell, as if reluctant to tell them the result of his call. He said, "You've got a week. Drews, the Governor says he wants to see you and Whipple as soon as you can get to the capital. Now I've got to go out and tell these people the show ain't coming off today."

Bentley plodded back to his office. Drews grinned as he held his hand out to Cobb. "It will be different when I get a new trial for you."

Cobb shook hands absently, his gaze following Bentley until he disappeared. Cobb said, "You sure done a job on him. His face looks like a piece of beefsteak. God, I wish I could have seen it."

Drews moved toward the door. "You can relax now, Al."

"I reckon." He hesitated, then he said, "Linc, you got pretty well acquainted with Janice, didn't you?"

"Yes. I've known her for four years, but it was just a proposition of meeting her on the street and I'd tip my hat and say, 'Good morning, Mrs. Purvis,' and she'd say, 'Good morning, Mr. Drews,' and we'd go on our way. But in the twenty-four hours since she came to my office, I've learned to know her very well."

"I missed my chance with her," Cobb said glumly. "I ain't fooling myself. If I'd taken her with me that morning when I left Fortune like she asked me to, she wouldn't have suffered the way she has. Neither would I. But I wasn't man enough to risk it. Maybe I just didn't want to be tied down to any woman, even one I loved. Now it's too late. I know it and you know it, and I reckon she does, too."

"She said she'd come and see you if you'd like," Drews said.

"No, I don't want to see her. Too much has happened for us to ever make it together. I guess I love her now, but I wouldn't if I had to get out and hold down a job and look after her and Jerry. I'm too old to change, Linc, so just leave it this way. Tell her not to come."

"All right," Drews said.

"But she's got to have somebody," Cobb said. "Somebody to love her and take care of her, and try to make up for all the misery Ronnie gave her." He paused, studying Drews as he chewed on his cigar, then he asked bluntly, "Do you love her, Linc?"

Drews hesitated, wondering if Cobb had meant all he'd just said, and decided he did. "You don't learn to love a woman in twenty-four hours, Al, but I could, I think. I'm sure of one thing. She's going to be a different woman in the future than she has been. I think she discovered something when she forced herself to come to my office yesterday morning to help you. She found courage she didn't know she had."

"Love her," Cobb said passionately. "Marry her. Make her happy. She never had no more chance than I did."

"It will take a little time," Drews said, "but I'll do all I can to look after her. And some day . . . Well, who knows what will happen?"

He left the jail then and walked rapidly toward the Purvis house. Janice would be anxious to hear what had happened. He thought about her as he climbed the hill, how she had lived in her own private hell for so long. It would take a good deal of time for her to forget it; she would have to build her life over, be given the tools with which she could build, and that, he thought, would be his first job.

Center Point Large Print
600 Brooks Road ● PO Box 1
Thorndike ME 04986-0001 USA